Chapter 1

The coil of a truck convoy slithered through the desert, silent in the early evening twilight. Radios gave no chatter, leaden eyes stared straight ahead. The convoy had been running for three months now, every Wednesday reaching their base of operations around 9 pm.

A crumble of falling sand in the rocky landscape beside them brought the lead truck to a halt. Grumbling exhaust pipes rumbled down into the stilted, rusty chugging of a dust wave, blanketing back along the vehicles that caused it.

"Visen." A single word clicked out over the radio. A woman in camouflage-laden cargo pants slipped out the back of a troop carrier three trucks down. She scanned the night before and around their convoy through thermal googles with all the precision of a sniper, eyes glinting back and forth between the crevices she knew could best conceal a man.

The trucks weren't allowed to fire a single gunshot in self-defense; that would cause an international incident. But Visen could at least make sure the path ahead was clear of IEDs.

The Republic of Mertria had taken to planting IEDs along their border with Livonia just last year, slowly and ever encroaching into territory in which they had no right to plant explosives, precisely because they knew this convoy was up to no good, passing as it did from Livonia into Mertria— they simply didn't have the infrastructure or intel necessary to catch the trucks red handed.

But Visen hailed from Mertria herself, so she knew precisely how Mertrians planted roadside bombs, and what to look out for. "Section clear." She radioed back to the convoy's lead truck, after about five minutes of pacing.

She'd get to disembark and repeat that procedure about ten more times before they reached the convoy's last unofficial checkpoint, a dingy scouter's outpost of malaria flies, sweat, and half-flickering fluorescent lights, right on Livonia's border with Mertria.

Under cover of darkness, they trundled past the unmanned barricades into Mertrian territory— though any manned Mertrian outposts further on down the road would be able to tell, if they were spying hard enough, by the fuselage shape, and the cumbersome back-flaps on troop transports, that these trucks were Livonian military.

Even Visen wore the equipment assigned Livonian scouts, though her shoulders remained suspiciously void of any ranking insignia.

Two miles on, they finally halted, 20 more soldiers in Livonian dress stepping down from truck cabs and tailgates, to help park and unload the crates of smuggled munitions that were their responsibility for the evening.

From here, it was a question of pack mules, though the threat of IEDs dropped off considerably, because, heading straight up as they were, into the rocky slopes of Livonia's steepest landslides, there were simply very few places left to successfully bury landmines.

Snipers, though, would still be a problem. Mertrian snipers weren't particularly good at their jobs (except for Visen), but Mertria, as a new Member of the Swiverlian Federation of Nations, had recently been granted a set of military grade drones to help survey their land in search of potential places to attempt agriculture. The Mertrians had, of course, instantly begun using the drones to help pinpoint munitions smuggling instead, because, by this point, smuggling was really the only thing keeping alive an insurgency of over 3,000 revolutionaries hiding out within Mertria's newly semi-autonomous borders. —That was the thing about joining Swiverlia's Federation of Nations; you were forced to become only "semi-autonomous." The military grade drones were meant to help sweeten the deal.

Mertria's insurgents had begun revolting about six months after their country's switch to semi-autonomy, demanding an economy that actually benefited the majority of people living in Mertria, among other far flung fantasies.

Now, one of the munitions smugglers clad in Livonian military garb, who went by the name of Colby Briant, sweated placidly through unloading guns from the Livonian troop transporters, with one hand to his neck, just in case drones were about—there'd been rumors Mertrians had rigged them to shoot convoy members.

He checked a tallied list of individual serial numbers, recording every gun meant to be smuggled over to Mertria's insurgents, while soldiers saddled bundles of semi-automatics onto a fidgeting row of donkeys.

82 old T578s were all the Livonians could afford to give Mertria? Really?

Hadn't Livonia recently received all-new ammunitions from Swiverlia? —Livonia had been a member of the Swiverlian Federation for quite some time now (of course they had been; they were always beating Mertria to the punch).

Colby thought it a bit uncharitable.

Officially, of course, Livonia wasn't giving anything to the revolutionaries' efforts, except a promise to help stabilize the region after whatever coups were necessary had been completed. And even that they'd only worded as a glisteningly innocent promise to promote favorable trade with Mertrian businessmen, should the Mertrian government ever look more favorably on trading with Livonia. (The current Mertrian government wasn't inclined to trade with a neighboring Autonomous Republic in the habit of actively undermining their sovereignty by smuggling munitions to rebels.)

Of course, in practice, the promise to collaborate economically simply meant the Livonians would help Mertria get rid of the Red Cross.

Mertrians hated the Red Cross, because they were Mertrians and hated Swiverlian millionaires handing out patronage, which was essentially what they believed the Red Cross to be doing.

The Red Cross had actually come to Mertria long before the rebellions began, a product of neighboring Republics beginning to worry starving Mertrians might not have the best impact on their own GNPs, which had already taken a nose-dive when the Mertrians decided to stop trading with all their neighbors simultaneously. But, as much as all Swiverlia's other Autonomous Republics disliked Mertria, it would still be far worse if all the Mertrians simply dropped dead; for one thing, think of the smell.

So, they'd brought in the Red Cross, to save Mertria from its own lack of infrastructure.

The Mertrians claimed the Red Cross stole all their jobs. The Red Cross, that is, and several other charities that had been brought in as well to combat rampant administrative problems, which mostly stemmed from the fact there was no centralized administration in Mertria to speak of.

These charities were all bureaucracy and stupid rules, like forbidding the storage of vaccines in refrigerators that were perfectly functional, just because the refrigerators happened to have Coca-Cola logos sprawled up their sides.

It was enough to talk about humanitarian shortcomings; when local cultures' idiosyncrasies weren't hurting anyone, to change them by force became colonialism— and it turned out keeping their Coca-Cola refrigerators alive and kicking proved the proverbial hill of a principle Mertrians gladly would die on.

Colby's pack-mules wound silently through gullies and escarpments, trailing ever closer, by the aid of memorized maps, to a rendezvous, the location of which changed every gun-run. Down the slopes Colby inched, picking at the subtly slippery rockfalls of a passage which didn't quite constitute a trail, down towards the silent, feeble glow of a single, isolated— Red Cross station.

Seriously? The one organization in miles capable of summoning international condemnation and the insurgents decide it's a good idea to come draw electricity by tapping its wires?

The pack mules and their human counterparts skirt sneakily round the aid-camp's soft pool of light, praying no insomniacs on the volunteer team chose this exact moment to go to the restroom. But it was midnight by now. Nothing stirred under the floodlights.

About five meters of surreptitiously camouflaged contraband wires for siphoning electricity off to one side, and Colby found the silhouette of three Mertrian rebels, waiting with checklists, ready to receive their 82 T578 rifles.

They led the small team that included Colby silently on into the bowels of a cave where, after three left turns down sloping tunnels, thanks to the inadvertent generosity of the Red Cross, blindingly white fluorescent lights enabled insurgents to unload the weapons they hoped would eventually force the Red Cross to leave. The irony and idiocy of modernity was not lost on Colby Briant.

"You've got to be careful you know; they'll catch you," he side-eyed the rebels almost mockingly (all Livonians and Mertrians spoke basically the same bastardization of Swiverlian, though, in fact, Colby was as much a Livonian as Visen; they actually lived in the same Mertrian city).

"We've been doing this for months."

The contraband electricity wrapped its way expertly up the side of a stalactite-ridden wall.

"Every time you see us the electricity's Red Cross; they're the only ones who have electricity anymore,"

"Yeah fuck the Red Cross,"

Colby had the distinct impression the insurgents blamed the Red Cross for a failed infrastructure that was, in fact, entirely the fault of insurgents blowing things up.

"What's so bad about the Red Cross?" he laid out 2 more T578s for underlings to take off to stockpiles, a tad grumpy.

"They're just a cover mate, for Livonia to take over all our shit,"

"We're Livonia," Well—technically they were Livonia; they were wearing Livonian uniforms. "And we're helping you."

"No, I'm not—no I'm just saying; we're friends; we're friends; I'm just saying NGOs are shit—'s stupid,"

"I feel like those they help would drastically disagree,"

"Will you shut up," a third gun runner passed Colby, mouthing less than subtly.

"No I'm sure they don't even—" ungrateful insurgent #1 hmphed at the weight of lifting 10 T578s all at once into a securer position behind an outcrop that doubled as his bed—"sometimes I'm sure they don't even realize they're doing it; but they cripple our infrastructure," he puffed to pick up another load, "which is precisely what Swiverlia wants them to do."

Oh sure, just because he was fifty years old and had a beard, he clearly understood global economics. Colby continued unpacking silently. If insurgents were pissed the Red Cross controlled daily necessities, they ought to aim at providing a viable alternative, instead of blowing people up.

Colby, obviously, was comparatively new to the gun-running business. He still had leisure to disagree with pre-established assumptions, even if he knew the disagreement would do no good. All this tripe was just what higher-up revolutionaries told subordinates. A parroting, to make them feel better, like they were part of something noble: '*The Red Cross is stealing our infrastructure!*' Oh sure. And hospitals spontaneously exploding was the work of shoddy contractors; no insurgency involved.

Colby stuck an unnoticeable black square to the barrel of the last gun he handed over and took comfort in the relief of knowing they would soon be back to discussing tactical maneuvers. That was his specialty, tactical maneuvers, not warped politics. His ability to explain T578s was why Ivle had requested he accompany this delivery to begin with.

"Alright," Colby stood in front of the group, contrapposto, once all the guns had been put away and the insurgents settled into awaiting his presentation. "This. Is a gun. I assume everyone knows what that is." He'd been hired to explain the range and usage to which T578s could be put, as long as insurgents promised not to target civilians. Which was like leaving a cat in with a canary, but Colby didn't want to lose his job and Ivle could make that happen if he dared to point out discrepancies.

The barrel of the gun to which Colby'd attached the black square had faded ominously into darkness, placed at the far back of a dimly lit side room.

It left Colby feeling lonely, somehow, counting down the minutes, as he strutted, reviewing bullet velocity for a crowd that looked like it knew both exactly what bullet velocity was, and how very much they would like to use it to get Colby to shut up.

But bullet velocity was important. These assholes get the bullet velocity wrong, they take down one of their own men three meters behind the target. "You can't think of these as some cool punk's weapon, yeah? You have to respect. The machine."

The fifty-year-olds watching him stared silently.

"This? This can punch through walls. Like I'm talking serious plaster damage alright?"

Everyone knew that.

But it was perfect timing, because at that precise moment a searing fluorescence punched through the cavern's front entry way, illuminating their entire ensemble. And it wasn't coming from the Red Cross.

Of course, the only functioning administrative body that still had electricity left, besides the Red Cross, was the Mertrian government insurgents were rebelling against.

Chapter 2

Colby was the first to put his hands up, squinting sideways to try to pick out silhouettes amidst the floodlights; he'd been told to cooperate—the rest would follow suit. Then there was nothing but shouts, purposefully rough handcuffing, and standing in line, to solemnly swear again and again: "Livonia. I come from Livonia."

That was all Mertria needed to hear.

This was clearly an act of war.

Smuggling weapons to insurgents was an act of war, and the Mertrian government would retaliate. Conventional treaties between Swiverlia's Autonomous Republics be damned.

All along, Mertrians had known Livonians helped erode the authority of their president. Now, they had proof; physical proof! They could even track the mule team back to the Livonian border, because someone had been stupid enough to keep chain-smoking cigarettes. It was circumstantial proof, but it was proof, dammit! Also, one of the captured donkeys had replacements for hoof rot made out of plastics from a Livonian company.

Livonia could say someone had stolen their officer's uniforms all they liked. Hell, Livonia could say refusing to let the common Mertrian citizen trade with his Livonian neighbors constituted an oppressive regime— that was precisely the sort of half-baked interpretation Livonians kept whispering to Mertrian insurgents, apparently.

They could say Livonia stood for freedom and justice in the face of irresponsible tyranny and the Mertrian government would still call for an amassing of arms, with a very sweetly phrased "training exercise" that just happened to take place across the border from where Livonia's defenses were weakest.

Because if Mertria did strike against Livonia now, they had all the proof they needed to show the world their attack was nothing but a defensive measure, against systematic encroachment by a government that used insurgencies as a fifth column to undermine Mertria's constitutionally assured autonomy!

Livonia's Prime Minister, Krakoveen, was all too well aware of this fact. He'd received news of a tracking device, that, having somehow been introduced amidst top-secret operations, enabled the Mertrian national guard to trace a clandestine arms smuggling operation headed by Livonia, about which Krakoveen himself had never before been informed.

A telegram warning him had arrived about two hours before the Mertrian high beams actually turned on to disrupt Colby's presentation, and Krakoveen had spent the rest of the evening sitting at his desk wondering how the hell he was going to excuse what Mertria was about to discover. It wasn't like he had time to warn anyone—even if he had known who in his cabinet was responsible for breaching about eighteen different peace accords— because if Mertria's border defenses weren't exactly the strongest—and they weren't—Livonia's ability to communicate with agents beyond that sparse Mertrian defensive network was practically nonexistent as well; the convoy was on its own now.

This was, perhaps, why the two antiquated, dethroned empires disliked one another. they were both a bit behind the times, and hopelessly aware of the fact.

Krakoveen drank whiskey over ice and had no idea who to call for help. The UN had already sanctioned Livonia into oblivion for a slightly less clandestine arms deal they'd tried making with Mertrian insurgents the year before. (Note: this had occurred six months before the Mertrian insurgencies officially began, which may explain why the UN was so skeptical about the entire process to begin with).

Meanwhile, the United States wasn't interested in the affair because they were the only country Mertria currently liked trading with, and they wanted to keep it that way. And France (a traditional Livonian ally), was very quietly wiping its hands of the whole affair. Of course, France had been after the land that comprised both Mertria and Livonia for years, but you didn't see the UN sanctioning them!

Krakoveen's phone rang.

"Black Ops reports 250 ton-trucks merging down IF1." (Interfederal Highway 1). 'Ton trucks' were troop transports. The 'training exercise' had begun.

"Also,"

Livonia had one little harbor.

It now had seven submarines blockading its entrance.

It really was a pity the Livonian president had to be so old. And so bent on secretly executing anyone rumored to disagree with him.

Krakoveen had suggested the Livonian merchant-marine needed to be replenished a good five years ago. But no, funds had been redirected to supply educational facilities instead, where teachers taught inane mathematics to country bumpkins who would have no use for it in real life, even if they were to move to the cities.

Krakoveen quietly tallied off the seven ships currently in Livonia's harbor as most likely laced with Mertrian explosives already, even as he talked over the phone, and sent out a communique for Livonia's three submarines remaining beyond the small periphery of the state's one aquatic outlet to stay put for heaven's sake and try not to breath too loudly (it was well known that what Mertria lacked in border defenses they made up for in underwater surveillance, via a single splurge the government had made a while back on a thing called an Isometer, which could ping wavelengths across the ocean and pick up all sorts of clandestine operations, with the additional feature of having not been overly expensive to purchase).

The Livonian president had also declined Krakoveen's requests to purchase their own Isometer last February. Which meant they were now relying on where the bubbles from Mertria's poorly built submarines could be seen surfacing in a semi-circle round their harbor, to count how many subs were actually being used to blockade it.

The Livonian president, of course, was being alerted to developments at the same time as Krakoveen but was graciously allowing the Prime Minister to deal with all their unpleasant repercussions.

Livonia's Ministry of Defense, meanwhile, was being surprisingly reticent when it came to sending out troops, because they wanted to see what would happen when the none-too-popular Prime Minister was finally overridden by the President, who would, undoubtedly, make a very stirring speech to all the Mertrian warmongers at the last moment and make sure all this nonsense simply went away.

It was Livonia's Ministry of Defense, you must remember, that was feeling friendly enough to supply weapons to Mertrian insurgents to begin with. And there's no better opportunity for a coup than the open window provided by a distracted military. Several higher ups in Livonia's defense ministry were hoping this would be the night that led to a rekindling of trade between Mertria and Livonia, which would mean a great increase in the worth of all those mutual funds used to house their pension plans.

Meanwhile, the total tally of 250 ton-trucks became 386.

"If we retaliate," a Minister of the Interior kept reiterating in hastily scrambled together cabinet meetings, "it will look like the beginning of war; we've got to go about this thing delicately, and slowly."

They put the Livonian air force on alert and called the UN to beg they broker a peace deal. The UN began convening a quorum to vote on whether they could in fact broker peace deals regarding Livonia. This may have been against the bylines of their agreement to sanction countries that helped terrorism.

By three AM, ministers throughout Livonia, regardless of subcommittee, had been sweating into the cradle of their desk phones for an average of about 26 calls a minute, and the supply of comforting cigars and glasses of whiskey was starting to run low.

It was now that Krakoveen called a friend, a very good friend, a very old friend. Maybe the one man in this life who still understood the world was run by human beings; still knew a glass of whiskey shared in times of turmoil could be worth its weight in gold….

Chapter 3

Evelle Ivle the Second, of Ivle & Ivle Incorporated, was woken at 3 am by the erudite tinkle of one of twenty-six faux ivory desk-phones his wife had actually had the audacity to purchase for every single one of his vacation homes.

He rose to flick on a light and put on a bathrobe.

"Mmmm... darling what time is it?" the form of his much younger wife shifted in bed beside him, perfectly manicured legs curving over luscious folds of silk. "Don't answer it; come back to bed,"

—Something about this reaction irritated Ivle, as though groaning slightly was all Nadia was ever good for, and it felt like a slap in the face to know he had to work while she didn't. She ought to know better than to question his diplomatic prerogatives. He picked up the phone.

"We've got a problem." Krakoveen didn't need to introduce himself. He had a particularly nasally voice, besides which Ivle had the distinctly bureaucratic luxury of being able to assign a different receiver to each individual phone line he cared about. The receiver connected directly to Krakoveen's office was kept by Ivle's bed.

Livonia's Prime Minister explained the amassing Mertrian forces.

"Must be an exercise. Manikai just sold them the IV49s—"

"No. We know about that too."

Ivle's intel, when it came to other country's military secrets, was almost always disconcertingly on point.

Krakoveen explained the Livonian faux paus of aiding rebel insurgencies and being subsequently caught in the act.

Ivle sat up at that.

"Now I know you know Badmonkof." Badmonkof was the president of Mertria, "Tell him there's been a misunderstanding. Tell him we'll negotiate. Just get him on the phone now!"

"I can do better. Can you meet me at my place in forty minutes?"

"Yes."

"Alright." Ivle was never one to waste words.

He managed to invite Badmonkof over using even fewer.

Then he got out of bed and turned on the overhead light. Badmonkof's cooperativeness depended entirely on being able to find mimosas and whiskey available upon request at all times. Ivle began scribbling a list of favored liquor brands to telephone down to the sous chef in charge of the kitchens after nine.

"Eechh," his wife stirred lethargically to cover her head with a pillow.

Ivle continued writing.

"Evel-le; it's too late to do work;" (she had no idea what he'd just been told over the phone), "come back to sleeep,"

"Yeah," he smiled, judgmentally pained in his grimace and left the room.

Thirty minutes later, he was watching, from the sweeping lawn facing his mansion's driveway, as Krakoveen's sleek Mercedes wound its way through the night, followed ten minutes later by Ivle's own personal lawyer, Jacobsan, in a Jeep.

Jacobsan was something of a family friend; he knew all the family's secrets, even Ivle's extreme irritation with his current wife. And for some reason he always managed to make every interaction feel comfortable and calm, by never passing up an opportunity to talk about golf.

By the time Krakoveen had gathered up his briefcase and thoughts enough to join Ivle and Jacobsan, where they stood waiting for him, the wind had gathered into swirls of an unnatural degree; Badmonkof's helicopter was landing.

As soon as he saw Krakoveen, the chubby, suspicious little Mertrian president balked. "Oh no. No no no. Is this what it looks like?"

"Does it look like a last-minute attempt to negotiate?"

"I don't negotiate with terrorists."

"Then now's the perfect time to tell them so."

Badmonkof felt betrayed. He'd been under the impression Ivle was about to suggest one of his patent political intrigues, which, Badmonkof had hoped, would cement relations between Mertria and Swiverlia (Ivle's home country), to the detriment of Livonia.

"You're a turn coat,"

"I'm a diplomat; that's practically the same thing," Ivle grinned and led the three of them, plus one of the assorted residuals Badmonkof always dragged along with him, into the darkened, eerie confines of his mansion. Suited, as it was, to Mertrian sun, the house now seemed to stand vacant and staring, idle on its lot.

"Krakoveen himself asked me to call you," Ivle stepped back from Jacobsan and the Livonian Prime Minister, to catch Badmonkof alone in an aside, "he says it's all a terrible mistake; which means no matter what's happening, they're backing out now,"

"You did this didn't you? You're an imperialist!"

Oh god. So completely Mertrian. "You always think someone's trying to take you over; when will you learn no one wants that crappy little plot of land?"

"Don't you—try that—I trusted you! You're a Swirvelian just like the lot of them! Fuck you."

"Okay,"

Ivle turned to include the other three once they'd all settled into a conference room (this may have been Ivle's vacation home, but that didn't mean it couldn't support business). "So, I've called this meeting because I don't think we need to let the peace we've been fostering between Livonia and Mertria peter out," — There was no peace; there never had been any peace; both countries were continuously re-arming, waiting for the other side to strike first. "Just because we can't agree over something so entirely fixable—"

By 'fixable' Ivle meant they could always simply agree to join forces and get rid of the KAVOCEN insurgency itself. KAVOCEN stood for 'Kill All Venomous Oppressors of Common Mertrian Nationals.' At least the terrorists were fairly straight forward about what they wanted to accomplish.

"Livonia is selling arms to KAVOCEN." Badmonkof's junior assistant had a habit of twitching his neck like a pigeon when pissed at having to point out the obvious.

"And that's what's entirely fixable."

"Even the UN sees arms-running as a breach in international security conventions."

"But since when have you ever sided with the UN?" Evelle ignored the yuppy Mertrian and turned instead to Badmonkof himself. Mertria had three outstanding counts of genocide that weren't about to just magically disappear. The UN steadfastly refused to let Badmonkof join their little world-economics club. But he wasn't about to let Ivle side track his resentment.

"Look, I know what an invitation to war looks like," Badmonkof hissed. It looked about like 386 ton-trucks heading towards Mertria.

"But that's just the thing; Krakoveen is saying this isn't an invitation to war—it's just a—just a military exercise,"

"Oh, you really think we're supposed to—"

"I'm sorry," Ivle interrupted the yuppy, "what's your name?"

"Johann Smutt."

"Johann. Can I bother you to go get a large bottle of Krasiberg whiskey? I had my kitchen master leave one out specially."

"I've come as the foremost Mertrian theoretical politician."

Mertria was so behind the times when it came to enlightened politics, they'd actually combined what ought to have been a common strand running throughout informed decision making into a single bureaucratic post to save time. "And I have some vitally important statistics we need to—"

"Perfect, thank you; yes, we'll take a look at that," Evelle snagged Johann's briefcase out of his clutching, pinioned posture as though doing him a favor. "2nd door down on the left. Then you want to take a right. Then a left. Then another right. Go down two flights of stairs. Then turn left."

He needed to get rid of Smutt.

He got rid of Krakoveen next by asking him to go retrieve his own "amateur—you know, just curious—" (and far more accurate) equivalent to Johann's analytics from a very far away home office.

He needed to get Badmonkof alone.

"What are you trying to do?" He turned on the Mertrian president as soon as everyone else had left the room (Jacobsan, in his capacity as lawyer, didn't really count as an entity separate from Ivle). "Spook Livonia into a war? You really think you have the moral high ground here? You know how easy it would be for me to call up my friends in Washington, right now? You think a few guns are worthy of starting a war? Because I'm sure Washington's equally interested in knowing what happened to those thirty billion or so tax-payers' dollars that just—conveniently disappeared, right about the time you put in that new jacuzzi." (It was a very expensive jacuzzi).

"That's domestic—and it's slander; that's none of Washington's business—"

"It is when 6 billion of those dollars came from American corporations."

There were only two American corporations that had managed to set foot on Mertrian soil in the past fifty years. "A bit steep for a tax hike, eh? 50%? Isn't that about 20% higher than the taxes you've been letting Krakoveen's countrymen get away with?" (There was, of course, some illicit trade between Mertrians and Livonia despite official sanctions).

"That's 'cause the Americans can pay; it's proportional taxation!" (No, it wasn't; not if you looked at the incomes and assets).

"It's against the Avoi accords."

"Alright. So what do you want me to do?"

A knock.

"Hey," Johann had miraculously returned in under five minutes. He somehow managed to get back before even Krakoveen did.

Krakoveen had been to Ivle's office dozens of times. Probably snooping around.

"Alright, thank you," Ivle took the whiskey from Badmonkof's yuppy. "Mm… no glasses," he somehow managed to make this look like Smutt's fault. "I tell you what, let's go to my office, shall we?" Krakoveen'd been gone long enough by now. Ivle'd never been very generous when it came to accepting excuses like 'oh, I got lost' when it was clear his so-called friends were spying on him.

"Just, along through here," he shepherded, leading the way back across atriums to the private, discriminating folds of lushly tasteful decor that made up the more personal quarters of his house's east wing. "It's cozier—" and far enough away to allow Badmonkof's worries about what Ivle'd just said to sink in while they walked over.

It was a cool spring night, but there was nothing particularly rejuvenating about the faces and briefcases that followed Evelle now (they took Krakoveen's briefcase along with them), clopping down echoing halls in a little huddle, like a miniature bay of political speculation souring under the flap of their own trench coats, each of which appeared to have been cut into precisely the same high-shouldered snark, as though specifically chosen to be as intimidating as possible.

Surprising Krakoveen at obviously unofficial investigations was just the sort of political intrigue Ivle loved. He'd been born into this life, as the son of a Swiverlian senator. It was all so uproariously easy, to retain his signature, unflappable finesse. Of course, one had to have been born into the right milieu. You needed to train since birth for this sort of thing— to know not only spreadsheets, but live and breathe the gossip that was political machination, the minute strategizing of every country in a 3,785 mile radius —and for any country outside that radius, Ivle let subordinates fill him in.

Ivle's native Swiverlia was a bit of a cross, between Switzerland and Russia. They governed their far flung Autonomous Republics in the quaint safety of knowing no other nation could penetrate their mountain ranges, and sought to simplify politics by siphoning administrative responsibilities off to regional commanders so they could focus on industry, only instead of coo-coo clocks their largest export was a series of anti-personnel systems produced by the seventh subsidiary over which Evelle ruled as silent partner—and if you don't think you can rule over a company as silent partner, you've clearly never met Evelle Ivle.

Evelle was excellent at manipulating his home country's international relations, without lesser Swiverlian cabinet members ever knowing. He'd secretly been controlling Swiverlian politics for the last seven presidents in a row now— that was simply what experts would call doing business.

Now he led his guests through an open colonnade to the steps of a private back stairwell, then through a coded entryway, up into his private office, pouring the Kraisberg whiskey, as soon as he got the chance, into an array of crystalline glasses to set before each of his guests.

Krakoveen had, of course, been caught snooping. All the other politicians were polite enough to pretend to turn a blind eye. Ivle didn't need to say a word.

"Um. Smutt, do you mind guarding the door for us momentarily? I'd really been hoping this would be more of a, you know, closer chat between old friends, just, a quick catch up really; I'm sorry; do you mind? I've got some very friendly guards; you can debrief them on the statistics, and they'll go over it with me later," he handed back Smutt's briefcase.

No one said anything to contradict. On the contrary, Badmonkof and Krakoveen simply stared at Smutt expectantly.

Smutt seeped out, breathing poison in his fantasies, to go sit on a bench facing the office door.

"They got above your security clearance?"

"Don't worry; happens all the time,"

Turned out the door guards actually were pretty friendly.

One, in fact, was a newly repatriated Colby, let out from what ought to have been a life-long sentence for smuggling weapons by a few rapid phone calls from Ivle.

"Ok, so, like I said," Badmonkof snapped back into smiling a nastily solipsistic self-awareness as soon as Smutt left the room, "what exactly is it that you two want me to do?" (again, Jacobsan, in his capacity as lawyer, didn't really count as a 3rd entity), "You want me to just go lay down outside and wait for KAVOCEN's crackheads to get me? Is that what you want?"

Honestly? For Ivle? Yes, that'd be perfect. But if Badmonkof was asking what to do, even if he still sounded like an asshole, that meant Ivle's implicit blackmail about those American tax hikes had struck a chord.

"No, that's what we've been saying all this time; that's what we've been trying to say; we can work together to stop KAVOCEN; we don't like them any more than you do, that's coming from a Swiverlian, and the Livonians,"

"The Livonians are selling them guns!" Was Ivle not listening?

"No! What we have here is a third-party armament purveyor! It makes no sense otherwise."

"And they were just…wearing Livonian insignia."

"Yeah. To make you do precisely what you're doing now. Think of it; why would Livonia want to go to war with you?"

"—riding in Livonian armored trucks."

Badmonkof needed to overlook that little detail if the negotiations were going to work.

"Ok. No. They were just pretending to be Livonian. I can prove that." Ivle'd been the one to supply them with the fake Livonian uniforms.

"It was black flag ops,"

"Probably United States,"

"—or UN peacekeepers—"

"That's—same, thing I just said."

Badmonkof eventually whittled them down to 'rogue Livonian general'—who Krakoveen would liquidate as soon as possible (he was already mentally culling lists of all the pacifist idiots at the Ministry of the Interior who'd thwarted him earlier that evening).

"So, you can see it's a one off, you don't need to worry about this happening again."

Badmonkof did worry about this happening again.

"It's not Livonia's fault Mertria has atrocious border security!"

"It is Livonia's fault we have atrocious border security!" (Livonia'd run black ops destroying what little border security Mertria had three months ago).

"You know, it really is the border security that's the problem here, isn't it?" Ivle paused philosophically.

Badmonkof didn't like how their self-proclaimed mediator was so obviously aligned against him. "It's not the border; it's the fact they keep crossing it!"

"Livonia can help you with that border security. Y'know? I know precisely what to do. We give a peace offering. Livonia gives a peace offering to Mertria; the whole region benefits."

"I don't need a fucking—"

"No, listen. They give—Livonia gives—you. A brand new border security defensive detection system."

"Wait what?" Krakoveen was looking between Ivle and Badmonkof, essentially putty, by now, in Ivle's hands.

"Your new detection system."

"Right." Krakoveen hadn't wanted anyone else knowing about that.

"Why don't you share your knowledge of those computer networks with the Mertrians. That way, we all see Livonia really does only want what's best for their neighbors."

The defensive network was an entirely new type of computer system, invented by the 5th subsidiary over which Evelle reigned as silent partner. In fact, unbeknownst to either of the two politicians sitting across from him, Ivle actually stood to gain 50% in proceeds if he managed to successfully sell it to anyone.

"We can't afford—" (that was Krakoveen, for Livonia).

"No, Mertria pays for it. You just help set it up; intellectual property sharing,"

"But, we can't afford—" (that was Badmonkof, for Mertria).

"Of course you can," The jacuzzi hadn't been that expensive. "To preempt war from occurring again? To keep your insurgents from getting the help they need? Your country'll be stabilized within a month without those gun-smugglers; and no need to invade, because Livonia is by your side—"

"No, I mean I don't think we can afford to let Livonia know all about how our defensive systems work!"

"No, they'll just be training your men! Ivle & Ivle'll be the ones who actually encrypt your system! It's a great idea!" Evelle was forced to jump on his own bandwagon, when Krakoveen hesitated over his whiskey just long enough to prove he didn't like the plan either. "A peace offering," Ivle ground out at Krakoveen to remind him. "You're not giving away secrets; your people just help install them; gesture of good will." Also, it would cost Ivle's subsidiary 820$ less for every man-hour they didn't have to provide their own workers.

"Alright."

It was agreed. Mertria could feel safe in the promise of internal peace, Livonia avoided a retaliatory invasion, and Evelle Ivle the Second walked away 3 billion dollars richer.

In fact, there was only one person who remained remotely unsatisfied with the evening's tribulations, and that was Johann Smutt.

All his forms and preparations had been ignored in favor of playing good old boys. "I tell you what," he eyed Colby about half-way through his wait outside. "You ever want to make some money?" he stood up and walked over to Colby, taking out his business card. "You let me know if he gets up to anything," he nodded sideways at the oak door to Ivle's office, "I smell a rat, you know what I mean?"

"Ivle's perfectly above board,"

"Yeah, yeah I know; you're trained to say that." Smutt'd known the other guard— a bloke named Wheeler who didn't seem very smart— would come out with something like that. "Just. Call me." He nodded at Colby.

It wasn't possible for there to be so much egotism in a single room without somebody wanting to double cross someone.

Unfortunately, the oak door was, in fact, remarkably thinner than Johann had realized. He thought he got out his last meaningful smirk at Colby right before Ivle's lawyer surprised them both by clinking open the door to exit, having finally overseen the signing of papers ensuring Mertria would get their new defensive system from Ivle's 5th subsidiary by September 18th—the three men now remaining inside the room were subsequently arguing over how exactly Mertria was going to pay for this. Ivle had graciously suggested perhaps Jacobsan should get the ball rolling by putting through their newly signed order form while he and Badmonkof were still ironing out smaller details.

True oak having gone the way of deforestation's popularity in the late eighties, Jacobsan had therefore been in a position to hear Smutt's every word to Colby from the opposite side of the door, before he'd even gotten a chance to open it.

Certainly explained the not-so-subtle-as-intended eye contact between the two of them, when Jacobsan did exit the room. No wonder Ivle didn't trust this Smutt guy.

Jacobsan, for his part, knew enough about Ivle's personal life to start several small wars, if he wanted to. Divorce had a nasty habit of inspiring wives to let out all sorts of unsolicited, confidential information, and Ivle was just gearing up for his seventh divorce in a row (he got bored very easily post-marital vows). Jacobsan would have to let him know Colby's loyalty might have been compromised.

Chapter 4

Ivle returned to the purely domestic stairwells of his villa that morning at 9, feeling cocksure and calm. This was how the world was supposed to work. Those who actually understood what was going on, discussing things civilly. Oligarchy was just an ugly name for the only system of administration that actually worked.

"You were up all niiight; what were you doing?" his wife came over to kiss him (she didn't want a divorce. He was worth 12 billion dollars in back taxes alone).

Ivle never really fantasized; his closest approximation was a certain self-awareness that incapsulated his whole reality in the comfort of knowing he could slip into expensive dock shoes at any moment should he want to, but whatever it was he was doing in his mind at that moment, he found himself entirely interrupted.

"Ivvle?!" it started as an explicative at knowing he wouldn't answer, then twisted up into a question, to not seem too irritating.

"Business! Just, business."

"Well, are you going to pay attention to me now? I made breakfast."

"Thanks."

She'd supervised the chef.

He took a single bite of toast, smiling to exhibit appreciation and headed off.

"What no snuggly time?"

"Ah, no I've gotta—" follow up on ensuring regional peace—.

"I got my nails done in that new color you like," his wife plowed some sort of polyester claw collection down the middle of her blouse.

"Yeah, looks great; I'll—see you in a bit,"

"Ivle?"

Oh no, she was following him— "But you didn't even look at them,"

"I'm—'nother time, okay?" *Eesh*—he had to call Colby—.

"You ingrate." he could hear her muttering soon as the office door closed between them. "I slaved away on these just for you and you didn't even look at them! These are 16.50$ an hour for these nails!"

Oh my God.

Yes, 16.50$ an hour of Ivle's hard-earned money. (How did it take longer than an hour to do someone's nails anyway?)

How was it even possible someone could be so self-absorbed? Was this normal for twenty-something year olds? Ivle couldn't remember being twenty-something; he doubted he ever had been.

"And I made breakfast!"

Ugh. She'd been doing this more and more lately, getting more and more demanding—and less and less attractive as she went. Because no matter what people say, Ivle knew: personality does matter.

He called Colby from the miniature office he'd retreated into to save time, warnings of Colby's potential infidelity received loud and clear from Jacobsan.

"Bravo 1? This is Eagle—" Bravo 1 was Colby.

"Oh no you don't!"

Oh—Nadia *actually* snatched open the office door; she'd never done that before. Ivle'd told her explicitly this space was off-limits.

"Yes sweetheart; please? I'm working—"

"Is that that bitch you've got running around for you—?"

"What?!"

"You're calling her, aren't you?! I knew it!"

So, this was how Nadia thought she could win back a husband. Wonderfully attractive, really.

"No, I'm not! I'm calling—what are you—?" *O-oh.* She must be thinking of Bravo 2, the Mertrian sniper, Visen—the one Colby'd been eye-fucking all weapons drop (even Ivle could see that, through the tracker he'd had Colby plant for him).

"No, sweetheart, I'm not talking to a lady! Ok?" He was always more responsive when other people could hear him; made Nadia look like a freak. "This is Colby, you remember Colby?"

"No! No; don't you try that shit on me; I remember that moniker!"

It was so ironic because Bravo 2 was literally the only woman in the world Ivle had absolutely no interest in cheating on his wife with—

"You're sleeping with her, aren't you?"

"No! She's a dyke! And she's got a face like a— literal dyke—"

"Oh haha yeah very funny lemme see the phone—"

"What?! No! Nadia. Look, I'm not calling her— I won't—!" he hung up on Colby. "Ok. See? 'Bravo 1' is gone. Okay? Now I'm calling Colby, okay? Happy? You remember Colby?"

"No."

She supervised him dialing.

Honestly, if anything was going on, Nadia was probably the one sleeping with Colby.

"See? Same number. Hello? Colby?"

"Sir? I don't think—"

"Are you Colby? Verify yes or no now."

"Yes!"

Ivle shrugged at his wife until the loud-enough-to-be-speaker-phone confirmation shuffled her on her way out the door. Even then, she only really gave up because it was so obviously a male voice speaking.

—That was the only kind of argument Ivle didn't enjoy fighting (the extremely stupid kind).

"Alright Bravo 1."

"Sir I don't think it's best on an insecure—"

"Yeah, I know; sorry about that; she's just getting—oddly paranoid. I've got a job for you."

According to what Jacobsan had just told him, Ivle wasn't particularly worried, even if insecure phone-lines did compromise Colby's real name, whoever might be listening in. Agents were plentiful enough he could afford to get rid of one who might've been contaminated by Smutt's attempts at bribery.

But he reverted to code for all aspects of the job. That part couldn't be compromised.

"I'm sending you a packet."

Colby wouldn't know what was in it.

"Monte-March. Be there at 8."

"I heard Monte-March!" his wife shrieked through the door.

"Nadia! For Christ's sake!"

He didn't dare mention Colby would be giving the package to Bravo 2—the very Bravo 2 Nadia loathed. He sent that by encrypted text instead.

Chapter 5

Monte-March was code for the closed subway station at Jubilee Avenue. It was one of the only places in the Swiverlian capitol that didn't have 24-hour CCTV surveillance. Colby let himself down through an uplifted grate, then waited in the darkness; two minutes—five—. A form trickled towards him through the shafts of moonlight iron grating overhead slanted across the disused tracks.

The form nodded. "Follow me."

Colby could only acknowledge. It was dangerous to talk more, even if they were the only two men within those five miles of unused subway tunnels. He had to show he took their mission seriously. Silence was a courtesy to other, unofficially snooping lackeys like himself; it showed respect for one another's concerns.

So, the two crept silently through the tunnels, halting alongside one another for the informant, Bravo 3, to point towards a fork in the track they were meant to take to the right.

"Two-pronged exit," he smirked, with a nod of his chin upwards to show he meant this as an explanation.

It didn't even occur to Colby that the meeting place he himself had chosen might be better suited to the act of ensuring seclusion. He knew better than to question. Life working for Ivle made agents furtive, dull, and dead eyed. But Colby could tell this Bravo used to be a special agent for some government. His instincts were still honed, his soul had simply died out long ago somewhere, like a snake sloughs off skin. Probably ex-Swiverlian CIA, Colby calculated. Or FBI? Or would it be in Ivle's best interests to let such higher-up specialists keep their jobs?

In fact, the alley Barvo 3 had chosen to traverse was the only one in two miles that could actually be seen by passing L trains, but these only passed once every seven minutes, the first and only train to interrupt them rumbling by undisturbed just as Bravo 3 handed over his consignment: a small, metal tube, which, when rattled, produced the faintest sound of a USB drive being clanked from corner to corner.

"So," Colby raised a quirking expectation through his brows, to avoid asking incriminatingly obviously questions like "where to next?"

"Parking Deck, Herb-Alpha," Bravo 3 nodded, "You meet to exchange."

"And I carry back?"

"Same size."

"To?"

"Logan." Logan was Bravo 4.

"Alright."

Bravo 4 had a regular drop site. Ivle's operations were thickly entwined enough even multiple subordinates active within the same city couldn't assure all exchanges promised a second face present to ensure goods were properly received. Colby would have to trust Logan's faux postal box (that was the drop-site) had successfully maintained anonymity these past few days. The box disappeared every so often, only to reappear a few weeks later in another section of the city, keeping postal masters off their toes so no one ever had the time to double back and check on why they had a feeling that collection box wasn't supposed to be there.

Bravo 2 was already waiting when Colby arrived at Herb-Alpha. Visen looked beautiful, as usual, even if she did look sleep deprived.

This compatriot, unlike Bravo 3, was worth breaking silence to talk to.

They had more important matters to discuss than the evening's dull business, if Colby was any judge of a beautiful woman's assets. He just needed to draw her out.

"I know you from the stakeout the other night, don't I?"

"Sorry?" a pulse round Visen's lower jaw wheedled a faint sign of worry through her muted gaze. She preferred to avoid being compromised every bit as much as Bravo 3.

"The Livonians?"

"Yeah? Maybe?" she checked for watchers. "We're gonna need a busser," —a moving car, to talk unhampered. The code agreeing to keep communications simplistic promised Colby'd understand.

But he didn't follow her till she turned back to check why he hadn't. "There's one three basements to the left from here," he was supposed to know to follow her. "Come on,"

"Oh, I see; well, why don't we take my car, it's closer anyway; you don't wanna go all that way—?" he was about to say 'in heels' (that was his go-to ribbing of a subtle complement) but of course, Visen wasn't wearing heels.

"That's—just orders; we go in this car; you're to use it for your next assignment."

Ok, so she was a bit dull round the edges, refusing to acknowledge the way he bounded just an extra tad of excitement through the way he spoke to her. He shrugged to come up alongside her, like he'd found some secret humor in having to follow.

"So, you wanna tell me how a nice girl like you gets caught up in something like this?"

"Hm?"

"We're supposed to act casual, right? So, act casual,"

Oh God; he was so formulaic, though. Visen almost died of second-hand embarrassment; who cared if he was clearly trying to pass off the formulaicness as a joke.

"Ah. Right. Well…"

—But if Visen carried on pretending she hadn't noticed he was flirting, this sort of thing almost always escalated.

Then, there was no way to stop it but to be curt— anything else was seen as an invitation to continue.

And once she was curt, then the begrudging set in.

But one mustn't acknowledge the flirting straight on, either; Visen'd tried that before and they'd pretended they hadn't been doing anything, even to themselves, then blamed Visen for causing their over-reaction into feigned disinterest, by saying she was hard to work with, because she'd reacted coldly when they were just trying to be friendly.

Colby *was* just trying to be friendly, that was the worst of it. Simply— at a caliber where it precluded Visen from the teamwork that leads to efficiency.

But to poke at him for it, to have fun with it —to try for a friend overtop nature's conquertizing drive— that Colby would construe as encouragement. At least, others had done so before, enough times Visen had grown wary of trying again.

So, here she was, bound to a detached professionalism that, at one time foreign, had by now become her signature personality. Now she would get to mimic how she would act had she no forewarning from patterns she'd seen a thousand times before as to how this conversation would try to bend, and bend, and bend aside.

Polite little nothings really were Visen's own personal hell.

How'd she get into this line of work?

"Same way you did, probably,"

She was here because Ivle knew all about her, even that one report from higher ups that claimed she'd gotten a bit too splash happy with a flamethrower, though it was, of course, what Ivle knew that higher ups didn't, which'd cost Visen her freedom.

"Oh?" Colby sauntered to show he was joking, "So, you were discharged from the Air Force with the highest honors a sergeant can receive?"

"Oh, no; I meant I met Eagle through work." There really was no guarantee these walls weren't listening. Best stay in code.

They reached the car. She opened the driver's side.

"Oh no, don't worry; I can drive,"

Really? "Okay." It was a dinky little Chevette.

She walked round to get in the passenger's side.

"So, what do you like to do when you're not getting in cars with strange men?"

"I don't know," Visen tried smiling, "this is more just a job for me —really," —Colby pulled past the A-frame barricade that rose upon paying 3.95$ for parking (Ivle's money). "Alright, now we turn left here for IF1."

She was waiting for when the roads had more lanes to start talking. She'd already cased the car, to ensure no bugs were listening in. But until they reached the highway, she needed to keep alert. She'd had concerns a previous job's Nemesis might still be following her. Luckily, it was much harder to ambush a car going 65mph amidst a bunch of trucks.

"No so I mean like what do you like to do? Like for fun?" Colby was casing their surroundings too; he was just more relaxed. "Like when you get a day off?"

"Oh; I catch up on sleep usually," They did only have about 20 minutes to exchange instructions. This was why small-talk always stressed Visen out; she never knew when it would end—

"Oh, so you like to sleep around?" Colby grinned.

He was 100 pounds bigger than Visen. The leissaz-faire attitude was now, officially, idly alarming.

"No, I mean I just find this kind of work tiring." She caught sight of a car that could be following them, made sure it turned off.

"Well, y'know, if you're ever in need of adventure—"

"Oh, no I meant more like physically tiring, not so much boring."

Alright, so this one was dead inside too it seemed.

"Ok, we want IF1 Southbound."

"Says who?"

"It's the drop location."

"I think IF30's a bit less busy this time of night."

"Yeah, that's why we need to take IF1; you're to drop me off around 5 turns after exit 378; we need to lose anyone if we can,"

"I'm dropping you off?"

"Yeah, at the drop location,"

"I thought we met to exchange,"

"Right, but then, afterwards—"

They hadn't exchanged anything yet. Visen was waiting for the open highway to do that too.

"Alright, so just, drop you off, right ready to go? Don't you think that's a little unwise?" Colby played the same smile over his face that he'd worn while warning insurgents not to get trigger happy. "It'll be dangerous,"

"It'll just be a party; I slip out the back." Visen'd slip out the side, but she no longer trusted so many questions.

"Ah, ok; this's what Ivle said?"

This was how Ivle always planned that sort of thing.

Why did Colby have to think it was cute to review the fundamentals of Visen's job with her? Or did he really think she didn't know? Now she sounded as though she truly believed the coy front, that he had no idea what he was doing. She just hadn't known how else to answer; she didn't want to acknowledge the coyness; she didn't want to have to worry about anything else right now except the difficult job for which she needed to prepare mentally.

"Alright, this is your package," as soon as they had merged onto the highway, she handed him an apricot sized lump in a well-done wrapping job, complete with 'Happy Birthday' printed on the paper, taken from a clip on the left strap of her bra.

"Ooh. I like this kind of present."

She acknowledged the joke with a nod.

"And from me to you," he handed over the USB.

"Thank you." She clipped it again above her shoulder.

"You like that?"

"I don't know what's in it." She tried to avoid registering the pun about fumbling with bra straps Colby hadn't quite bothered to put into words.

Silence.

Ok, so no jokes; she wasn't very good at reading jokes.

"You know, I was up at Ivle's house a few nights ago. He had the Mertrian President there, and the Livonian Prime Minister. I got to talk to them,"

"That sounds exciting."

Ok, she wasn't interested in that either…. She kept looking for any cars that might be following them.

"Yeah, there was this one guy there who just would not leave them alone; like he had all sorts of data or something; they had to make him go sit outside,"

"Oh, no…. Sorry, I'm— who am I supposed to give this package to?"

Jesus, what a robot. Couldn't get through to her.

"Max Liverton; he's staying in room 7B of the Livonian embassy in Mertria,"

"So he's one of the tech specialists they sent over?"

"I don't know." The feigned disinterest was creeping in, threatening to endanger Visen through sheer laconicism.

Visen sat cogitating what this might mean if she was caught. Max had to have something to do with that peace offering from Livonia to Mertria—Ivle's intervention had been all over the news. So why the secrecy about a final component? Or was this unrelated?

"Has anyone ever told you you ought to smile more? You look really nice when you smile."

"Oh—thanks; I thought I did smile—like—back there a bit,"

Ahah! Colby was getting through to her; that had been a bit of a smile now too! (It was pained, and the only form of reciprocation she could think of.)

"—Nah I was just— wondering if they gave you additional instructions on how I'm to access Max." These details were usually given along with the packages to be delivered.

"Oh; through Parvou's 'Northmost' park."

"But—that'll be obviously coming from Swiverlia." Parvou Park contained the junction at which Swiverlian, Mertrian, and Livonian borders met. The 'Northmost' park was Swiverlian.

No one ever entered Mertria through those by-ways unless they were up to no good. Wouldn't Swiverlia look underhanded if—?

"Oh no, it's not like Mertria'll notice." Colby had failed to overhear Ivle's altruistic plans for bolstering Mertria's surveillance capacities, even with the permeable oak door. He'd been too busy watching Wheeler—the other guard—make an ass of himself trying to befriend Smutt.

"It's just I thought the whole point of these detours was to make it look like we came from Livonia," otherwise why were they bothering to drive her to Livonia?

"No Mertria's not gonna be able to pick you up,"

"But on the off chance they do that'll ruin the mission—"

"You don't know that." It was true, she didn't. Maybe Swiverlia wanted to look like they were taking an active part in Mertrian-Livonian relations. (Honestly, Ivle hadn't thought it through that closely; he'd figured: it was a park, what direction someone came walking through it surely didn't indicate anything noticeable enough to be damning). Visen usually knew better than to question orders, anyway; Colby second-guessing everything she did must've made her worry.

"Also, I mean think about it; how far is it from Swiverlia to Mertria's Livonian embassy?"

"Oh, yeah,"

He kept waiting.

Oh. Oh no.

That question hadn't been rhetorical.

"Ah, about half a mile I think," *Socratic method? Seriously?*

Visen was so sick of obvious explanations overlooking the point of her worry she didn't even bother arguing; that was simply what it meant to be professional in Mertria's armed forces.

"And how far is it from Livonia?"

"A—mile?" She checked side mirrors; answering obediently wasted the least possible amount of brain power.

"Right; so, see? It's the shortest route of access; Eagle wouldn't want you sacrificing anonymity; it's just the best route."

"Yeah," How was it possible to solve nothing so self-confidently? And how quickly could Visen change topics so he wouldn't feel invited to continue? "I'll go along Delfi's Cape, then." That was a cliff. Provided a bit more anonymity than any more direct route.

"Alright, yeah," Colby nodded along. Yeah, now she was being plucky; he liked that, defending unnecessary worries. "As long as you don't mind damaging your nails," he laughed.

"Yeah," Bravo 2 tried to react appropriately, but concerns over her own nails were so obviously alien to her she couldn't think of a polite trajectory along which to respond.

"Alright, this is exit 378. We're aiming for that farmhouse." Cars from other revelers were already parked down either side of the road; small gaggles of six or four passed them by, tipsying towards the party.

"Looks fun,"

Now to blend in.

"Right, ok pull up right here; —no this is far enough. Perfect. Thank you, Bravo 1." Visen unlatched the door, far too tired to be anything but politely professional til the end, despite unwanted advances.

Colby left thinking he was starting to get his way with her.

Unfortunately, he thought it'd be cooler if he drove off even after he heard a bit of a "—Colby!" right as he revved to depart. If Visen had second thoughts about wanting his attention, this was the phase in a relationship when such guesses ought to be let out to dangle for a little bit— frustrated, enticing.

His phone rang.

"You're to drive the Chevette to Coup-Charlie; and park curbside—spot 391 or as close as you can make it."

She'd meant that to be the last thing she whispered through the window as he left—that was why they'd parked as they had, secluded yet visible—otherwise it looked awfully awkward being let out at a dinner party without any departing words to the person who'd bothered to drive you.

She supposed, if anyone asked, their backstory now included having just gotten in an argument. Continuing instructions over a cellphone wasn't necessarily compromising. Enabling agents to pass on information over the phone had been why Ivle developed their elaborately coded vocabulary in the first place.

Visen walked up past the dusty farmland to a lantern-strewn porch. The party was a catered affair and after a polite greeting at the entryway, by someone else Ivle had managed to bribe or blackmail into pretending to know her, she headed, meandering, out through the gardens to retrace her way to a side street. Now for the hard part.

Chapter 6

The only problem was that Visen didn't trust Colby. It was like he was talking continuously to an idea of what she ought to be, and not to her.

Of course, this sort of thing had happened more times than Visen could count; she was simply one of the few women in Mertria's military. Occasionally, it was just harmless fun, a wink to let her know she was liked, and then at least she felt like it was a joke in which she was included, even if she wished desperately the older generation didn't feel such a need to acknowledge they knew this substrata of gendered identity hovered over every conversation like metadata—after all, if they didn't acknowledge it, it wouldn't exist.

Sometimes, the reflex to treat her differently was involuntary, and then her coworkers drew into themselves with a shyness like hatred. But Colby's reaction was almost worse—for one thing, it could so easily turn into the same unstated divide, if she replied a bit wrong, if she didn't pay attention closely enough—

But even before Visen failed to live up to expectations, turned Colby against her, of the three reactions to her existence his type was the most distracting, because it alone wanted to illicit a reaction, so she had to confront it, deal with the constant alternative to what they were actually supposed to be doing, which led, ultimately, into not taking her seriously enough to avoid putting her at risk, even if only with the subtle differentiation of refusing to engage in analytics about an upcoming operation. And then, when failure struck, people would blame Visen for not doing her job correctly.

No, since she'd mentioned Delfi Cape to Colby, she'd travel through Mertria's marshlands instead, just below Delfi, in case he mentioned it to anyone.

The marshlands might be safer anyway.

Ever since Ivle'd first approached Visen about working for him, she'd figured: if he knew her secrets, she'd keep tabs on him too.

She'd seen on the news how he'd brokered the deal for Livonia to help Mertria with new border defenses, and she knew, from researching Ivle, that Huntsman Security, the fifth subsidiary under Ivle & Ivle's umbrella corporation, had been churning out thermo-vision defensive hardware as their most popular export for the past two years in a row.

So, she assumed, if Ivle had brokered the deal between Livonia and Mertria, the border defenses he'd suggest using would most likely be his own.

Just to be safe, she'd studied up on these defensive networks independently, in conjunction with the information Ivle'd given her about this mission (some debriefing material, like which parts of Mertria's border were most heavily guarded, Ivle habitually avoided entrusting to two separate Bravos—which was always a blessing; it meant Visen got to read up on the briefing literature all on her own.)

Visen had correlated the briefing's particulars with information available in the public domain, so she now knew the defensive networks she'd be crossing on Mertria's border were indeed the same as Ivle sold, or, at least, a type almost identical. And she knew they relied on a particularly sensitive type of microbolometer to produce the live feed of whatever boundary they were guarding, along with how to short circuit that particular model's signaling capacities.

It did make sense the Mertrians were excited about this new technology; it'd certainly be a lot more effective than their current method of sticking day-time cameras at strategic locations and wondering why they failed to pick up any image when it was dark out; Ivle's subsidiary did make an incredibly efficient defensive system.

But, if Visen entered Mertria through the marshlands, she might be able to outsmart it.

Huntsman sensors were sensitive enough that Whil-o-the-wisps and other naturally decaying carbons would give off enough background heat to disguise her passing form as nothing but natural incongruencies, if she moved quickly enough, in line with the vapors she could see even now rising across the Mertrian border's steep valley.

So, with one last look over her shoulder, to make sure no one followed her, she set out from the north end of Exit 378's town.

Joshmen Ferry was a strange and narrow outcrop of residential zoning, with overly-bumpy speed humps promising the width and breadth of this small suburb petered out before reaching even half the length of one of the code-named segments by which Eagle and Bravos subdivided cities.

The town's last two houses, before the boundless plain, were a tiki souvenir hollow and a courtyard with Coca-Cola umbrellas for eating tacos under. The taco place was always closed.

Visen was pretty sure they were a money laundering front.

Out onto the cool savannah grasses she went, with no one to worry about except the coyotes, howling somewhere hopefully closer to the horizon than to her.

She snuck between cacti and rambled down cattle trails, working, almost subconsciously, on her backstory, should anyone catch her on this leg of the journey: she was stargazing, in hopes of finding the Nebula Orioso. In fact, she actually did hope someday she'd have leisure to look for the Nebula Orioso. But now was not the time, even if her pockets were filled with binoculars and star-maps.

The star-maps were to guide her home.

Mertria's border loomed closer.

From where she'd chosen to enter her home country, the demarcation between Republics looked like little more than a chain-linked fence, but the topographical differences were almost comically disappointing: from Swiverlia's savannah of wind-spun plants, to a pocket of marshy swamp, that sunlight could never fully reach round the Mertrian mountains to dispel.

She entered now a table-top-like land of plateaus and clogged rivers, bending by the nearest to run her hands through its idly tepid marsh waters.

About six inches below top-soil, exhaust ports fed into an underground tunneling system that housed the actual wiring and nerve stations through which Ivle's defensive networks broadcast out above ground the hatched lines of thermal-sensing infrared Livonia's display of 'good faith' had just helped install.

The exhaust port farthest from any heavily frequented joint of this underground maze could be found 25.3 meters due west from a nearby jutting escarpment known as Miramel Peak. (That was one part of the briefing Ivle hadn't relayed through Colby—just in case he'd taken Smutt up on his offer; didn't want Smutt knowing Ivle knew how to outmaneuver his own defenses)

Once Visen found the exhaust port—reaching through marsh waters to pry off its hidden lid—she'd be home free, because then the system could mistake her for the routine maintenance crews which came out every night from midnight till 5 am.

Ivle'd made sure they dispatched crew members to wander in solitude; after all, it didn't take two mechanics to fix whatever thermal detectors might have short-circuited during the day, and it wasn't like they needed someone to stand guard over each mechanic while they worked. They were already secreted away underground.

But Visen had to count on the will-o'-the-wisps running interference to get her close enough to slip off that exhaust port's cover and creep down— without the thermal detectors beating their 60% chance of error past 200 meters and noting her approach.

Luckily, Huntsman thermals were finicky enough, when it came to being over-exposed to dust and muck, that they tripped themselves for no useful reason a good three times a day too often for anyone to respond with any serious worry to the feeble alarm of 'potential incoming threat past optimal range' that one sensor, 25.3 meters due west of Miramel Peak, now began to read out.

Visen was gone before Livonian techs could re-scan the area where she'd been standing, to reassure the night shift's attentive Mertrian interns they hadn't seen anything worth reporting.

At 1:04, she punched in the key-code another informant had provided and slipped in from the exhaust port's shaft, to the network's main hall, hoping the bulges in her pockets from binoculars and maps would look enough like screw-drivers—or whatever techs used to fix infrared sensors—to pretend she was just part of the Huntsman's crew.

She slipped down the hallway to a small side channel, from which exhaust ports leading out to the Mertrian side of the border could be found. Honestly, it was almost as though the system was designed to be permeated; some sort of discrete politique. In fact, the real intrigue came from wondering how on earth the grateful Mertrians hadn't noticed their new defenses were made to be infiltrated.

Visen slipped out into Mertrian marshland, border successfully crossed. Hadn't seen a single mechanic. They were probably all drinking coffee. That was how Mertrians always prepared to pull off all-nighters: drink coffee until the night was over, and then hope there hadn't been anything else they were supposed to be doing. Honestly, when Visen had first joined the SEALs, drinking coffee was practically all her superior officers ever seemed to do.

She located the Livonian Embassy easily enough. It served as a sort of dual-purpose Check-Point Charlie, located, as it was, about a mile in from the more authoritative, legal, entries into Mertria. It really would have made much more sense to come from Livonia. Passports and excuses were easy enough to manufacture, but Visen supposed Ivle knew what he was doing. He always was about three steps ahead, compared to what he let his underlings know about the plans they partook in.

Max's Room 7B would be along one of the repulsively Brutalist cement outcroppings that snaked out from the Livonian embassy's sides.

Ah, yes, of course. It was right on the end.

Whoever'd built the place had conveniently labelled each room in large bronze lettering on the stucco wall that lined the right side of each apartment's miniature balcony. This was, in fact, to assist in evacuation procedures, but it made identifying 7B wonderfully easy.

Visen'd been wondering why they told her to follow a path which'd have her going over the embassy's west wall, in particular. Evidently, Ivle'd managed to get his hands on a copy of the Livonian embassy's floor plans as well.

She hoisted one foot over the mesh grating of a culvert that was meant, apparently, to keep revolutionaries from lobbing incendiaries in through the drainage. Everything else about the wall was equally easy to climb, done up as it was in easily graspable stucco.

Her gloves broke at the glass shards waiting pointily atop its ramparts, winnowing them down into something not too crunchy, over which she could hoist her body in silence; no tinkling of falling glass to be allowed. She brushed the shards gently to one side, working entirely by feel, then swung over the ledge.

But she didn't hop down. She hopped straight onto the terrace to room 7B and knocked on the French window separating the room from its side porch.

"Hello; excuse me are you Max Liverton?"

Max had been watching television.

He sneezed, "Hey, hey, yeah, come on in,"

She handed him the tube she'd brought, to watch him take out a small USB.

"Should we check and make sure it works before you leave?" he covered another remarkably wet sneeze by ducking the bottom half of his face through the neck-hole of his shirt.

"Yes please; good thought."

Never hurt to find out what exactly Ivle was up to. For one thing, he had, apparently, bribed a bona fide defensive software developer.

Visen could see Max'd been tinkering with code she recognized from the print outs she'd memorized, in case she needed to reprogram a few thermal sensors' alarms, to get through successfully.

"Okay,"

Max wore the kind of white socks that go up past the ankles and look bulbously scratchy even from a distance.

"So, what we have here…."

They waited for the zip file to download.

"Do you want some soda?"

"No thank you," the less things touched the better.

"Alright, so: here, we've just gotta, insert this there, and—" he typed some code, proffered by one application, into another application, running simultaneously, and started receiving output from a third window that may only have been the second application running in two windows at once.

"Awesome,"

Visen knew better than to ask if this was supposed to show the software was performing correctly. Instead, she tried to look wary, reading over the output like she knew exactly what she was looking for, to keep him talking.

"So," Max pointed to one of the windows, "these should be the encrypted codes from Mertria; that's what we'll be running back through the Aplidex; we're just translating them here," (another window).

Visen really didn't like how Ivle kept all his plans compartmentalized so successfully. She had no idea what an Aplidex was.

"Alright. And you have instructions on how to reach the Aplidex?"

"Yes, yes. I've already been briefed."

"Ok, good. Thank you, Max,"

"Thank you; good night." He went back to watching TV, to wait for the USB to download, feeling embarrassed he'd never gotten her name, but far too scared to ask her for it. That might be against protocol.

Visen liked working with people like that. They made your job easy. They were respectful and quiet and got the job done.

She slipped back out the way she'd come in, as instructed.

Mertrian Guards patrolled this area, most likely to impress the Livonian consulate with an aggressive expertise that didn't actually exist.

Their standard issue flashlights swept the thermal sensory grounds to Visen's left. (Why they thought it necessary to do this, when that was literally the only stretch of ground their new border defenses already monitored, was beyond Visen).

10 yards, though, and they'd be between her and the nearest vent she was meant to escape through. Visen blended up against an embassy wall, waiting for them to pass on and hoping the shadow of palm fronds that played up against the wall's stucco could hide her.

The nearest guard bent suddenly to stare at the ground in front of him. He seemed to have discovered footprints. Another shone his light towards the light in Max's room; it was the only proof around of someone awake at this time of night. They seemed to be inspecting Max's patio, then the ceiling fan in his living room.

How on earth would shining a flashlight into a lighted apartment help discover anything? Barely viable police states were so stupid. Visen skirted round to one side, further into the palm fronds, glad Max was too distracted by the TV to notice he ought to be freaked out.

But still, to get across the street… Ivle didn't seem to have thought of this step. Or maybe she'd finally done one too many missions and he meant for her to get caught— and subsequently "taken care of." Bravos' operations were usually timed to avoid security patrols…. Maybe Colby'd simply forgotten to tell her about a timetable he couldn't fathom being important.

She took out her binoculars and unscrewed a spare lens. She'd have to be lithe. She might manage it.

She cupped a hand over her penlight and flicked Morse code flashes of reflected light against the far chrome of a thermal venting behind the guards, making sure to catch the light against their eyes.

5 seconds for them to inch forward and attempt analyzing the message, 5 seconds for them to realize they ought to be focusing on where the light was coming from, and Visen had disoriented them enough she could slip past in the dark while they were rummaging after her previous position through the palm fronds.

One hung back, though, to see if the Morse Code would start up again. She had to hit him on the side of the head with her binoculars.

Could be worse. They could blame a sneak thief; that would mean less paperwork.

He crumpled with a low thunk almost in the same motion as Visen threw herself into a culvert ditch beside the thermal venting.

"Potters!"

She disappeared into the venting, a slight grating sound giving away her mode of exit.

Now, to run for it, as fast as humanly possible; they wouldn't be able to alert headquarters in time to track her thermal print through the maintenance systems. She just hoped moving so fast wouldn't automatically arouse untimely suspicions.

In fact, she moved so fast the system's 'internal maintenance hallway' read out in the control room— which was also being interpreted by Mertrians-in-training—was taken to mean there had been some sort of serge in the circuitry, and a night crewman was dispatched just as 3 guards (minus Potters and his medic) burst in through the same vent as Visen.

This did strike security as cause for alarm, and a special patrol was sent out to waylay whatever ragamuffins were wandering aimlessly round the venting region with guns, to keep them away from the more sensitive, top-secret thermal equipment.

Visen slipped out a far vent, back on Swiverlia's side of the border, panting in the controlled semi-silence stealth operations had taught her. Then she went panting in semi-silence back across the quiet plateau.

Chapter 7

Ivle received news of her success the next day.

He was spending the weekend at a regional spa, being hammered in the back by people who claimed to be experts in Swedish massage. Patrons weren't allowed to eat anything other than a prescribed diet, which seemed to consist mainly of Parsley, and after-hints of some fruit diffused in water which had once, presumably, tasted slightly more like lemons.

Ivle actually owned the spa, though he'd never visited before. His lawyer had suggested expressing amiability towards at least some of a marriage councilor's suggestions, to help negate the final payout he'd have to settle on Nadia.

So here he was, eating Parsley.

Oddly, the spa allowed inmates to watch Newsweek by the pool, which Ivle would've thought one of the least conducive background noises for meditation. But it seemed to be doing wonders for his wife. She was soaking it all up right next to him, fast asleep.

He took to reading the TV's subtitles.

"We have been attacked! This is obviously a Livonian ploy!" A Mertrian official seemed to be arguing with 12 microphones simultaneously, as an explanation scrolled along the screen's bottom: *cyber hacks leak classified Mertrian defense protocols*—ah, good. That meant things were going according to plan.

Max had managed to transmit Mertria's decoded communiques to the Livonian Aplidex, using, in fact, the same Chevette Colby'd driven to its predetermined drop-off— but that whole wonder of organization was far behind Ivle now.

"Darling?" He slapped his wife's thigh, giving it a contemptuous little rub to wake her up. She did have lovely thighs. "I need to get back to work, okay?

There's been a development; see? Just now," he pointed to the screen, "we've been hacked; that's my company's name on the line—"

Actually, Ivle'd scheduled the security breach so news of it would break about three hours into the spa weekend Nadia'd planned. Anything to get away from dehydrogenated citrus water.

"I've got to get back—" he was already calling multiple subordinates: "Yes, get on it right away; I want to know how it happened."

"Some sort of a backdoor sir,"

"That's not good enough; I want to know exactly what we're up against. Who had access to the codes?"

"Might have been a Max—Liverton,"

"Well keep an eye on him; get Interpol involved; we want this quarantined, contained—but gracious, Charles; we have to be gracious; we've fucked them over, now let's be their best asset fighting it and figuring out what to do next. You hear me?"

Mertria'd been able to tell, from metadata surrounding the leak's traces, that Max had hacked their main defense computer through the filter of Ivle's new security protocols.

"Evell-le? what's happening?"

Oh no.

Nadia'd followed him again— with that chatty Brooklyn accent that got drawly when she was sleepy— out into the marble hallways he'd just been striding through majestically with large, imperiously fixing-stuff gestures.

"There's been some sort of a leak, sweetheart, I'm not quite sure what's happened," he tried to turn back round to bending all attention over his cellphone, "No. I don't think—yes Interpol! God, this is an International incident!" he wanted both Mertria and Livonia to feel the world was watching. "I want *them* to come to *me*! No I don't want—yes invite them!"

"You need to invite Interpol to our house?"

Ivle began to suspect Nadia didn't know what Interpol was.

"No, no; just leave this to me, ok, sweetheart? enjoy your weekend, alright?" He hurried upstairs to pack, Nadia following in full face mask, slowly so as not to upset the drying of her manicure.

Something about this fiasco struck her as suspicious.

Nadia could spot faux fur from twenty paces. She could spot faux leather from across three football fields. And now she was beginning to feel as though she'd spotted a faux excuse to get out of husband-wife togetherness time. There was something very fake about the way her husband scampered, as she watched him pack, with one elbow quirked against her hip, the better to accent, in the way they curved out to one side, the overly long nails she'd just done up.

"But if you leave now you're gonna miss all the detoxing benefits; you can't find dehydrogenated citrus anywhere else,"

"Yeah, Nadia; it's an emergency." Also, Ivle owned the spa.

He went back to rolling out drawers in search of his heart medication.

Why had she packed sixteen suits for him to wear? What were they gonna do? Change after every round of Pineapple Puree?

"Is this your—? Wait a minute—"

"That's my hair ointment!"

"Oh, right, here—"

"But this was gonna be a fun weekend; I thought you said we'd finally be able to spend some time together,"

"Yeah; I know; I'm sorry; it's an emergency,"

"But I thought; you know," she winced as though they weren't alone in the 349 square foot pent house, "I thought we were gonna use this time to start fixing our marriage," she'd bought a starter's kit for BDSM after reading *Fifty Shades of Grey*.

"Nadia," he turned on the suite's plasma flat screen for her benefit, "this means war, yeah?"

"…You just came up with this because you don't like hanging out with me, do you?"

"What? No, sweetheart; it's on the news, here," he turned up the volume to drown out any future accusations. He could almost feel staff members pricking up their ears from adjoining hallways.

"Mertria is now calling for reparations to be made, claiming the Livonian government used an international gesture of good will as nothing more than an excuse to infiltrate the defenses they claimed to be bolstering."

"We have considered a mole may be involved—"

Nadia muted it.

"They can't blame you for something two countries did."

"It's our security defenses that were successfully breached, yeah?"

"The one on the border?"

"Yeah."

"But you don't even understand how computers work," she ran clattery heels after him as he lugged suitcases off the bed and out of the room. "You're not gonna be able to help em fix it anyway!" Now there really was a maid watching them. "You just made this whole thing up to get rid of me!"

He tried to smile at the maid.

"You don't actually need to go!"

"Sweetheart. I've got —PR, it's PR okay? Don't want two countries going to war, right?"

Nadia noticed the maid judging.

She turned back to the open door of their bedroom, grabbed the remote, closed the door, and turned the television's volume back up again, unsure.

She wasn't alone in her suspicions.

Even as Ivle struggled down the spa's stairwell, intent on piloting Autonomous Republics to peace, at least one person in the Mertrian capital was beginning to think Livonia hadn't really been involved in this recent round of cyber-hacking at all.

Johann Smutt had been replaying information from every quadrant of national securities for the last 36 hours, even if it wasn't technically his job; scrounging, eating, and napping in an undecorated, vinyl office just off to one side from the large wood-paneled hallways Mertria reserved for actually important heads of state.

He had already cross-examined every maintenance contractor who had anything to do with Mertria's border in the past month, along with all guards posted in the border's general vicinity. He'd even interviewed Potters, the guard Visen concussed, to make sure every aspect of the routine breaking-and-entry Potters' team had reported was above suspicion (it helped that Max had been clever enough to file a claim someone'd stolen his wallet and prescription sleeping aids when Ivle asked him to provide some sort of excuse for Potters' contusion).

But ultimately, no, Johann couldn't find anything suspicious at all about the night Mertrian security defenses were breached, except one potentially unaccounted for maintenance worker, and something that could've been a will-o'-the-wisp, right outside a vent the maintenance worker then appeared next to a moment later. Of course, there were always glitches in the interior CCTVs. They weren't as important as guarding the border. But that thermal glow, right before hand….

Coincidence? Anyone else would say Smutt was reading too much into the Huntsman systems' well-documented margin of error.

But supposing he wasn't? If he wasn't, that will-o'-the-wisp didn't originate in Livonia. No, it came towards Mertrian border defenses from Swiverlia, precisely as Visen had feared someone might notice.

It was simply bad luck that the one person who did notice happened to be inclined to believe that if Swiverlia was involved, the suspiciously backhanded asshole of a Swiverlian who'd kept him from advising Badmonkof at that humiliating summit meeting just three weeks prior might be the one hacking his own systems.

Chapter 8

Two hours after the first news of cyber-attacks broke, Colby sat in the forecourt of a sweeping lawn overlooking golfing greens and sipping a Southern Comfort. Ivle liked meeting subordinates here at his country club, amid the lazy swishing of overhead fans. Time seemed slower, more relaxed. New York moguls might rush their business meetings into an impersonalized list of stats, but the real elites, the ones who actually ran countries, could always afford time for a cravat and carefully chosen words.

Colby was used to this sort of life; he'd grown up rich. But he was anxious anyway; he'd seen the news.

"They know they've been hacked; they know it's only a matter of time before—state secrets, or whatever, are blown; I say, if you're gonna—I just, I don't quite understand," Colby had a hunch Ivle must've facilitated the attack on Mertrian defenses. The timing coincided much too nicely with the night he'd handed Visen that mysterious USB.

And Ivle seemed much too smug about it all. He must've wanted to frame Livonia, by ensuring it was a Livonian engineer who actually downloaded the backdoor used to hack Mertria's military defense databases.

But if Ivle wanted to give Mertria a reason to go to war against Livonia, why go to all the bother of trying to patch up relations between Mertria and Livonia in the first place?

Colby still had shin splints from standing guard outside that summit meeting all night.

And he wasn't stupid.

He knew this could mean one of several things. Perhaps Ivle was simply working for Livonia. (The media had latched on to Mertria's official, automatic assumption that it was in fact, the Livonians responsible for attacking their computers—no other country would bother bribing a lowly Livonian engineer; no other country seemed that seriously interested in conquering Mertria).

Or, perhaps, Ivle was in the business of framing Livonia, for Mertria. They'd done that before. But either way, why not simply tell Colby their organization was working with Mertrian—or Livonian—higher ups?

"You've seen what I can do; you know I can keep a secret." Their fathers had been together in the Senate Caucuses of '89.

"What are you suggesting?" Ivle honestly wanted to know what Colby thought he'd figured out.

"Well. If you're gonna make Livonia look like an aggressor—or give them a chance to become a better aggressor—you've already done that; and you'll need more than just your expertise to know precisely what to do next." Knowledge of civilian defense contracts could only bring Ivle so far. And knowledge of civilian defense contracts was the only knowledge Colby knew Ivle possessed. Colby, on the other hand, knew the politics of their federation's multiple militaries, from his time in the Air Force. "Defensive contracting can really only get you so far." He decided to say it out loud. Unless— could Ivle simply be trying to secure more defensive contracts with Mertria?

Honestly, Ivle hoped to draw up additional defense contracts with both countries—Mertria and Livonia; they were both uncharted markets. But that wasn't what this was about.

"Now, I can tell you," Colby always did have opinions, "if you don't push a bit, right now, Mertria'll forget all about this; nothing drastically damaging's been leaked yet; they'll think they can patch it on their own, and your business, well—"

"That's fine."

Only 1/7th of Ivle's financial interests were invested in accumulating defense contracts from neighboring countries. He'd never told Colby about the 1/7th he'd invested in plans for Swiverlian expansion.

"So, you're not interested in Mertria buying your defenses?"

"I don't need to resort to underhanded tactics to get Mertria to buy my defensive software, Colby." Very insulting. What did he think he was playing at? Some sort of spy thriller? Ivle let the displeasure sink in. Then, "I want you to give a file to Marvin Crassburger." Crassburger headed the Mertrian defense databases that'd just been compromised. "It's on this," Ivle slid a floppy disk across the warbled glass table-top, secure in the knowledge that ease and the far-off sound of tennis balls popping against rackets were all he needed to hide planning his heist in broad daylight.

Colby pocketed the floppy.

"Alright. Now, you'll come back to my place for dinner, won't you? I've got to show you just what Marvin needs to do with that."

Marvin Crassburger, for all his black-mail-ability— he was, in fact, the crowning achievement in Ivle's arsenal— had absolutely no idea how to actually utilize the central intelligence computers currently under his command.

Ivle'd tried digging up dirt on those among Crassburger's subordinates who actually knew what they were doing, when it came to computers, but they were all interns, too freshly out of college to have made any life-altering mistakes heinous enough to utilize yet.

Their superior officer was the only window in. And Colby would have to tell him what to do.

Chapter 9

Ivle's Mertrian summer house was only about a thirty minutes' ride from his country club, when driven by professional chauffeur. It was, in fact, even bigger than the country club, but it had the inimitable drawback of including Nadia within its confines.

She'd telephoned to say she was going to forgo the rest of her weekend at the detox spa—to save Ivle money. Of course, if her husband wasn't there with her, there wasn't really much point in being there herself.

She claimed.

In fact, Nadia'd spent the afternoon keeping track of precisely how long Ivle lingered at the country club he claimed to be visiting as a means to meet up with, and subsequently yell at, whichever underlings were responsible for the compromised Mertrian security.

Nadia knew that was a lie.

She figured he was either fucking that one masseuse he really liked, or the country club's bank manager, and she was determined to find out which.

Ivle usually took his conquests back to their Mertrian summer house for a second round of erotic stimulation and dinner; he was very predictable like that. Nadia had only to wonder whether this time foreplay would include golf lessons, or straight up fondling one other into a closet at the very first opportunity.

She'd managed to catch him at all four possible permutations: masseuse, manager, golf lessons, fondle-closet.

Nadia had always considered herself especially gracious, to let Ivle have free reign with all these little indiscretions. And now she was the one getting slammed with a divorce! And Ivle wasn't one of those gracious billionaires who didn't mind paying alimony.

She needed to start taking notes, if she had any hopes for a high enough settlement to keep her in comfort.

And then, of course, he showed up at the Mertrian summer house with Colby —*seriously?* She'd been expecting that Visen whore, Bravo 1 or 2 or whatever it was—he'd used that blatant switch between code-names a number of times, Nadia was certain of it. I mean, what was this? Did he really only have two agents codenamed Bravo? (Honestly, he only had 5. Bravo was the designation used for underlings sourced out of Mertria's capital, in which Visen and Colby did, in fact, each own cramped, dingy little apartments.)

Nadia wasn't about to fall for this two-man thing again. Somebody with a vagina was coming to join them.

Either that or Ivle was secretly bisexual. Maybe Bravo 1—or 2—or whatever the fuck he called Visen—wasn't the Bravo Nadia needed to worry about.

She watched through a CCTV readout as Colby followed his boss, skirting round back to her husband's massively mahogany office. Of six studies Nadia wasn't allowed to go in, that was the most important one, just to the left, off the ground floor's entryway, up a flight of steps. There were no cameras in there. And visitors needed to get past a special keypad to be let in.

Nadia'd developed an easy mechanism around that, though: a hidden alcove in the wall that separated her bathroom from the tightly secured office. She'd installed the little place as secretly as possible, so she could spy and take notes, because this was the office into which Ivle always brought his new sexual conquests—it was simply the easiest to access. Paid sex and friends' wives could slip in directly through a side stairwell that led to a backdoor outside. And then they'd call cook to bring over dinner. And feel secure in the fact Nadia didn't know the keypad's combination.

She'd already noted the time; early afternoon. Now, all she had to do was wait to catch the stage name of whoever walked in next. So far, she'd already documented "Lavinia", "Persia", "Hopspur", and a "Sex Kitten"—so named for her role-playing abilities, and the only one out of the four whom Nadia hadn't managed to trace back to her original .com advertisements to request confirmation about Ivle's playtime in the form of a receipt.

Of course, this time, Ivle'd only entered his secure office to show Colby the precise order of actions he needed to undertake upon inserting the floppy disk he was to deliver into Mertria's central intelligence databases, via Crassburger's office computer.

Step 1: a downloading wizard would automatically populate, asking if Colby and Crassburger wished to continue. Step 2: ….

You see, Colby was perfect because he knew enough about computers not to be frightened by installation wizards, but he didn't know enough about electrical power supplies to realize he was downloading proof Mertria housed an undisclosed nuclear reactor—the fact it was undisclosed hopefully implying Mertrians had plans to weaponize it.

And should Colby heed the siren's call of Smutt's proffered reward for snitching? Well, Ivle'd seen this sort of thing before. Someone tempted a subordinate; here, Smutt tempting Colby. Just an offhand comment. Usually something about making a bit of money on the side. Subordinate thought about it, stewed in the opportunity to feel like James Bond. Then, usually, the subordinate would shop around a bit, go to some lower-level government servant they had no business talking to, with promises to sell 'information', trying to find the highest bidder.

It was, in fact, an inexcusable sign of inexperience that Smutt had assumed Colby'd ultimately remain interested in turning over information to him. Governments always paid more than individuals for that sort of thing. And Smutt's involvement with Badmonkof's government had to be unofficial. It was the only way he could've wheedled so easily into Badmonkof's confidence.

It was only fear of official government channels finding out about plans to plant blueprints that worried Ivle. What could Smutt do, if Colby did leak him information? Whine some more from the other side of a locked cabinet meeting door? He specialized in theoretical studies; nobody'd take him seriously; Ivle'd make sure of that.

He'd just have to make sure Colby didn't deviate off to some lower-level government clerk entrusted with delivering pay-out for information tendered Mertria's intelligence services, when he went to go bring Ivle's floppy disk to Crassburger.

But Ivle would be sure to know if Colby did try to betray his plans. He knew right where Crassburger's rooms were located; and he'd brought Colby here to stick a tracker in him. So, if Colby didn't travel directly to Crassburger, Ivle would know. Then, if he did find Colby'd been turned, he'd make sure this assignment was Colby's last.

"So, then you move this file, into the database marked Cuwave 1. To do that, you open the database; it's a basic compilation of electrical resources—I want you to put these papers in the folder marked Mendol County." God, it was so easy to frame a country when their entire infrastructure only covered 36 miles.

It was simply bad luck that Nadia'd recently been watching a documentary on renewable energy, which included lots of ominously panning overlays—set to ominous music—of diagrams which looked exactly like the ones that popped up on Ivle's computer screen now. She definitely recognized that conical, penis shape on the blueprint. It was the thing the interviewer kept repeating was no good for the environment. She could even give a layman's explanation of how it worked.

She rocked back onto her haunches, from where she'd peaked out through the interior, cupboard side of a faux keyhole through which her hidden alcove looked out from one of the drawers built into Ivle's study's wall.

She wanted to give Ivle the privacy he deserved, if he really was just discussing 'business.' She didn't want to be *that* wife.

But why would they be adding blueprints for a nuclear power plant to what had to be a list of Mertria's internal assets? She knew Mendol was a county in Mertria; she knew Cuwave 1 collected lists of Mertria's internal assets; she even knew Crassburger was the one in charge of the database Cuwave 1, because Ivle forced him to come to dinner parties to keep him intimidated, and Cuwave 1 was the only thing he could ever think to talk about.

Ivle hadn't built any nuclear power plants in Mertria recently. Mertrians traditionally got their power from windmills.

"Now, this is just a simulation—" she could still hear her husband through the wall, but she didn't want to move until he and Colby had left the room; she was afraid she might make too much noise. "But you can see, in the real data base, it'll be exactly the same—"

Why did they need to practice on a fake data base before adding something to a real database? Why not just practice on the real data base? Did they not have access to it? Wasn't that the database Livonians had just breached? Maybe it was just a procedural thing.

"Won't they be able to disprove—?" Colby trailed off.

"Not before Livonia gets nervous."

So, they were planning on the Livonians seeing the nuclear power plant. And it sounded like that nuclear power plant didn't actually exist. So, were they... trying to make Mertria look cooler than it actually was?

Oh God, Nadia already *was* 'that' wife! But it wasn't like she actually understood what Ivle was up to; if he didn't want her spying, he shouldn't be so covertly sneaky all the time about business deals that were perfectly above board—

Unless—was this illegal? Oh my God! Had she been right to suspect they were acting suspiciously furtive?

Oh my God. Is this why people didn't trust businessmen? Was that stereotype true? Was her husband doing something illegal?

What the fuck was he doing?

She put her eye back to peer through the drawer's faux keyhole.

"Now the password for this bypass is 789animal; you have to by-pass that mainframe, so it looks like this has been in place for at least two months."

"Why?"

"Because it has been in place for two months."

Oh, she knew that tone. That was Ivle's 'I'm lying to you because you're so sweetly naive' voice. Whatever else was going on, that nuclear power plant had not been 'in place' for two months.

So why would they put evidence of a fake power plant in a country's database of its own assets? Destabilize how much power the country thought it could make? And then, once they'd expanded past their actual capacities—sit back and wait for them to call in outside help? Ivle did own controlling shares in an electrical company…. But that wouldn't account for hoping Livonia got nervous, not unless that part was just some side project.

Actually, Nadia's conspiracy theory was far more nefariously intricate than Ivle's actual plan.

No, Ivle was simply hoping to frighten both Livonia and Mertria into crawling to Swiverlia for help.

You see, both Mertria and Livonia were carved from land that had originally been promised to Swiverlia by Mertrians and Livonians seeking protection 300 years previously. You couldn't just renege on a 300-year-old contract. But that was precisely what both countries had been trying to do for the past 50 years.

If Krakoveen and Badmonkof came to Ivle for help this time, Swiverlia would simply increase her demands when it came to the price for protection. No more 'Semi-Autonomous Republics.' Not this time. No, this time, Swiverlia wanted full integration. Mertrian land could actually be very profitable, under the right jurisdiction. Ivle just had to make sure not a single aspect of his balancing act between regional powers went wrong.

Nadia backed out of her hiding place gingerly. She was definitely adding this to her list of divorce-able complaints.

—Then she'd get more alimony.

Ivle may've managed to 'declare intent' first, when it came to nullifying their marriage (—which was, apparently, a bad thing), but 'Planting nuclear reactors'?

That had to be more damning than adultery, when it came to allocating alimony. She'd ask Jacobsan.

Chapter 10

Nadia really did have the worst timing, when it came to popping off to take notes somewhere the scratching of a pen against paper would sound less suspicious. She'd left just a moment too soon. The minute she was out of her little spy nest, someone knocked on the window at the far end of Ivle's studio, facing the courtyard. Then, that someone slipped in through the study's side door.

Colby and Ivle really had hired an escort.

And they'd paid her 700$ extra to promise not to tell anyone they'd be sharing her.

Oddly enough, Ivle wasn't bisexual— at all. He thought that sort of behavior perverted, when it came to other men (course he didn't mind if the ladies wanted a little snuggle-fest he could watch). But he couldn't think of any other way to securely bug Colby. —Sharing hookers and actually trusting one another are, of course, completely different categories of friendship.

The tracker Ivle planned to sneak into one of Colby's orifices was a new invention from Ivle & Ivle Defensive Industries, capable of being absorbed through soft tissue, but too large not to be noticed in food or drink. That was supposed to be one of its safety features.

Ivle managed to insert it in Colby's rectum with a convenient butt-plug. It was only slightly smaller than the tracer Ivle'd told Colby to put on the Mertrian weapons, but Colby simply assumed it was part of the butt-plug; it dissolved shortly thereafter.

The two men spent the rest of their time trying to one-up one another's alpha-ness, with the result that the threesome actually ended up being quite boring, despite their escort's best attempts to split her attention between the two of them (Colby's butt plug had been her idea; Ivle had simply capitalized on the opportunity). Of course, both men were so alpha the only person who'd ever actually admit to themselves it'd been a bit of a disappointment was the escort herself, who walked away with 2,200$, which meant it really hadn't been that big of a disappointment at all.

Ivle, at least, now had Colby thinking he was deeply trusted, without actually having to tell him anything, and now, of course, he could be easily traced, as well. This would be experiment #37, to see if Ivle's tracker was ready to be marketed.

But Colby wasn't charmed by Swingers. In fact, he had enough of the old-boy Protestant turpitude left within him that he saw it as a sort of weakness, to have married someone who clearly didn't satisfy sexually.

He left Ivle's house with a renewed sense of self-assuredness, because the escort had clearly liked him better—ever since he volunteered to use that butt plug (she'd brought it in hopes someone would try it on), while, back at the club house, his boss had clearly been flummoxed by the need to conceal information Colby so self-assuredly asked after.

Ivle'd been grasping at straws, if he thought this fling would bind Colby's loyalty. Ivle was getting old. Time, Colby thought, to pull a few tricks of his own.

~*~

By the time Nadia returned to spying on her soon to be ex-husband—she'd gone off first to sunbathe as per routine by the pool and eat some cantaloupe—Ivle was innocently tracking Colby's progress towards Crassburger.

She didn't know whether to be repulsed or aroused by his never-ending efficiency. Efficiency was why she'd married him in the first place. That and the money he efficiency produced. He did look very sexy, squinting angrily at the screen as the tracking device up

Colby's ass made it perfectly clear that Colby was not making a beeline for Crassburger at all, as he'd been ordered.

Oh he was in Mertria alright.

But Crassburger's office was in the left wing of Mertria's governmental palaces. Colby was in the right wing, amidst the pathetic, dingy sort of vinyl-hued offices they gave second rate politicians.

At least this proved the tracking device was extremely precise.

Ivle growled as he reached for his phone (sexy for a 60-year-old; Nadia liked 'em old). "Bravo 2? Report. Come in. I've got a job for you."

Oh so now he was ready for sexy time with Visen. Right! That was going in Nadia's report as well.

She didn't even wait to hear the rest of Ivle's phone call, just snuck off right away to make a list of things she could ask Jacobsan about. (Jacobsan was, after all, a family friend. She'd been asking him for advice about divorce proceedings ever since Ivle'd announced he'd be using Jacobsan to procure one).

"Are you anywhere near Jolinta?" Ivle drummed impatiently at the side of his desk, as soon as Visen confirmed her identity. Jolinta was Mertria's capital; it was near where Visen'd been born.

"No."

Didn't matter, she was only half an hour's drive away, in Livonia on business. (Both countries really were ridiculously small).

It took Colby the entirety of that half hour just to convince Johann Smutt they weren't about to download some obscure virus, if he would just let Colby put the suspicious looking floppy disk in his office computer.

"I haven't seen a floppy disk in years; I'm not even sure we have a—"

"You do." Of course Mertrian computers were still compatible with floppy disks.

"Alright. How do I know it won't affect the entire network?"

Mertria was small enough almost all their government's computers were on the same network. They'd recently made it wireless!

"It won't—look. I'll use a laptop."

Colby didn't really understand how computer networks worked.

"You can't do that, it's not compatible—"

"Shit."

Visen, meanwhile, breezed through the Mertrian-Livonian border crossing, making a beeline toward the derelict apartments she used whenever she needed to spy on Jolinta's governmental palace. If booming economy had enabled landlords to accrue enough disposable income to pay for security guards, security sweeps might have forced Visen to vary her base of operations. But this was Mertria. As it was, the governmental palace was the only building in that downtown square still actively in use. Mertria was going through a bit of a recession.

She got her sites on Colby easily enough, using thermal goggles and the coordinates Ivle'd provided to scan through the palace. Eagle'd cordoned Mertria's governmental palace into segments precisely the same way they'd organized coded phrases for locations in Swiverlia's capitol.

Visen was looking for the section of government offices Ivle called Delta-8.

Johann and Colby continued opening all the files on Ivle's floppy disk.

"He's working for Livonia; he's gotta be," Colby'd been looking over the files in his spare time, "it's the only way I can make any sense out of it; he'll plant some sort of proof we have some sort of illegal weapon, right? I mean, that's the only way I can make any sense out of it." From the way Colby kept tilting his head while staring at the monitor, even Visen could tell he was still secretly thinking 'what is that thing?' Again, not the most knowledgeable when it came to power plants.

But Smutt, actually, had recently been watching this documentary on nuclear reactors….

If those diagrams were what he thought they were, this whole thing seemed a bit above his pay grade. He'd been hoping for a nice bout of wife-beating or skimming off the top of tax returns, you know, usual things billionaires could get away with with impunity.

As it was, he didn't really know what to do about finding Ivle planned to start a nuclear holocaust. He had, though— as Ivle hoped others would too— made the logical leap that if Livonians thought Mertria had secret nuclear power, they'd assume Mertria had nuclear weaponry too.

Smutt told Colby he thought the files were blueprints for a power plant.

"So, he would plant these for Livonian generals to find, using the hack they've set up? It hasn't stopped yet, by the way, they're still being fed information,"

"Really?"

The Mertrians thought they'd patched all that up.

Or maybe Johann was just too low on the totem pole to be told when everyone with Top-Level Security Clearance was secretly panicking.

"Alright," Visen called Ivle back, "I've got eyes on him." She simply assumed Colby'd been caught by Mertrian security while performing some sort of drop off. "What do I do if he's in trouble?"

"Shoot him."

"Do I shoot whoever he's with as well?"

"No. That might cause an international incident."
Ivle liked adding fuel to the flames, but only when he'd had time to analyze every possible potential aspect of the outcome.

Of course, as Colby was an informant, Mertria would be forced to sweep his death under the rug. Wouldn't want the average potential informant on the street thinking Mertrians couldn't protect those who helped their cause.

Ivle could take care of whoever Colby'd met with later.

It just better not be that Smutt character—

Rumors suggested Smutt was getting very chummy with Mertria's President Badmonkof.

But he'd been invited to a Summit Meeting; he couldn't be this low down on the totem pole—not far enough down to be in the palace's right-hand wing, surely….

~*~

Visen's marksmanship training with the Mertrian SEALs had never really been big on providing snipers with spotters. It was just a Mertrian thing. Their snipers were more old school, of the 'make sure you aim really well and then pull the trigger' technique, which came from a rich cultural heritage of shooting at bears without using hunting blinds.

Visen shot Colby dead on her first try. Poor Colby.

Honestly, though, she hoped when the time came someone would be there to do the same for her— bullet through the brain, far better than torture or slow decrepitude.

Then she waited for what the thermal body shape that wasn't rapidly cooling off would do next.

It kind of fluttered around panicking for a few minutes.

Then Smutt ducked behind his desk. Desks don't actually provide protection against sniper bullets. Don't try that.

Finally, after about ten minutes, he reached an arm up to the top of his desk and dialed a superior officer. The floppy disk's files were still open on his computer. "Sir? There's been a breach in security, Intel is dead."

Intel was the code name they'd given Colby when they found out he was coming. Mertrians weren't very good at giving code names.

"Shit." Johann's superior hadn't realized this would be so serious. He'd been planning to pass on whatever info Johann brought in to 'PR Tacticians,' which was basically just a state-owned marketing firm on the 4th floor.

"What'd he give you?"

"I'm pinned in; the sniper might still be out there—"

She was. She waited patiently all day, eyes never leaving Smutt. She'd have to wait until he left the building, to snap a picture identifying him.

Honestly, after 3 pm Visen began wishing Mertrian SEALs were provisioned with a spotter, just so she could take a break for even a few minutes.

Instead, she watched idly through the thermal goggles as seven members of an emergency response team were called out to creep silently towards Smutt's door. She watched as the rest of the thermal activity on floors 1 and three were evacuated, and as the clump of terrified thermal outlines that'd flummoxed into the break room with the thickest door on floor 2—that was the floor Smutt's office was on—were eventually relieved from their emotional agony and siphoned downstairs.

She had to shift her position, when several anti-terrorist teams came sweeping the nearest buildings. But she never took her eyes off Johann. She simply sandwiched herself above a boiler in a closet through which she could still pick up his thermal imprint. Search teams opened the closet door, but they didn't think to look up, they just looked round either side of the boiler.

Visen was left free to watch as one emergency response team member shouted "Clear!" to another, in the second-floor hallway across the street, and two subordinates burst into the office under Visen's siting crosshairs, to rush Johann out of the building.

Now she had to act quickly. The teamsters and Johann had almost instantly caught up with the chaos of thermal imaging still pouring out of a side door to the palace's basement. Visen took off her mask, side stepping down round the boiler. Probably not the best place to hide; she was soaking with sweat. Didn't matter. She opened the door. Two sentries were detailed to keep eyes on this floor—a task made much easier by the fact that a demolition team had already smashed away all non-load-bearing interior partitions in this part of the complex two months back.

But the teamsters guarding the floor below were called out to help quell the panicked office workers pouring out of the governmental palace, so it wasn't long before two second floor security guards became one.

That remaining guard became binocular fodder.

Visen realized only too late that meant she'd developed a traceable MO. Hopefully wounds from the side of a binocular's grip weren't overtly unique enough for law enforcement to realize she'd been the same assailant who attacked the border guard Potters.

She slipped down into the stairwell, thermals back on to keep locked on the human puddle of panic that awaited her across the street. None of the thermal blurs had been allowed to leave. They were all being corralled into giving statements.

Visen snuck out a side window someone'd helpfully already broken, then milled into a side street, eyes on the side door towards which her quarry was headed, thermals back off now, or she'd look suspicious. Any second now—he should be coming—the crowding workers still came raining down the stairwell: official toady, nice blouse, panicked older man still holding a sandwich—two SWAT-team-esque bullet proof vests on either side of one little wheedle of a man, who looked like the subject of an un-instigated rugby tackle. Yes, that had to be her target. Timing and physique matched. He was also the first to be interviewed, with phrases like "were you hit? Was a second shot fired?"

"No, no I'm alright—"

"Name?"

"Johann Smutt."

Ok, there we go. That was all she needed. Ivle could look up all the records he needed from that.

Visen slipped down a blissfully empty—and breeze filled—side alley. They really had done a lovely job of clearing the scene, though there were policemen stationed at the end of every backstreet.

She couldn't help thinking that might be a bit overkill, for one solitary shooting—in a government building, yes, but not of a government worker. She managed to shimmy up a drainpipe and hop roofs instead. They hadn't thought to secure the roofs. Typical Mertrian.

She called Ivle from the safety of a chimney's shadow by the open entry to a pizzeria just below; her form and the cellphone's ping easily mistaken for idle chatter on a smoke break; Visen's uncle owned the pizza place.

"Eagle?" She actually was smoking a cigarette. To fit in with her disguise as a casual onlooker, of course. Not because she was addicted to them in any way at all....

"Bravo 2; burner phone?"

"Yeah." All her phones were burner phones. She couldn't afford anything else. Most Mertrians couldn't.

"Alright, so—"

"His name is Johann Smutt."

"Fuck."

Smutt. *Really?* That little prick? How the fuck had Smutt managed to make good his claim he'd get Colby money? They didn't exactly give lowly theorists a budget for eliciting denunciations of presidents' friends!

How had Colby even tracked Smutt down?

It wasn't as though Ivle'd never heard of business cards. But he'd had every burner phone Colby'd ever used tapped; or, at least, he had the call logs monitored to check for abnormalities; he wasn't paranoid enough to actually listen in on all Colby's day to day routine busywork. But there had been no abnormalities! Colby'd called no one suspicious! So how had he set this up? Ivle had always thought he kept his agents too busy to allow them the leisure of running to the nearest payphone and calling in political denunciations.

More importantly— what was Badmonkof doing bringing such lowly second-tier officials to one of the most important political interventions of the past century? Ivle felt insulted.

Worse, he felt as though his hands were tied. How much did Johann know? Had Colby gone in with a 'hey I know you need dirt on Ivle, and I've got it'? Or did he allow enough of a gap in specifics to breed reasonable doubt Ivle was even involved, if the whole thing ever came to trial? Ivle assumed, of course, the information Colby'd been trying to hand over to Smutt must include the floppy disk Ivle'd just entrusted to him— that and, most likely, various prescient details of subterfuge Colby no doubt thought himself very clever for having coalesced.

But Ivle was a very private person; they'd never find any hard evidence he was up to anything; whatever Colby might have claimed. That floppy disk, with its nuclear blueprints, could never definitively be traced back to Ivle, not unless they found the mother file required to remotely access its compromised contents, for the next stage in Ivle's now rumpled plans. But finding that file would require breaking into Ivle's secure home office, and even then, all proof that copy even existed was so well hidden he'd already survived seven such break ins, reputation unscathed— not even counting Krakoveen's unofficial espionage that night they'd put a stop to Mertria's 'training exercise.'

It was just— Johann. Nosing around for incriminating details like that in the first place. That wasn't normal behavior for lower-tier pen-pushers, was it? Even if Badmonkof did like going to art museums with him.

No, someone must have tipped him off. The question then became: who was controlling Johann Smutt?

If they'd narrowed in on Ivle so much as to successfully corrupt Colby— an agent whose extensive affiliation with Ivle ought not to have even been known, outside his duties as a door keeper— might they not be clever enough to identify some other Achille's heel?

Say, the wife? Who even now had been following Ivle around a spa insinuating she suspected he'd orchestrated the entire Mertrian data breech?

True, she thought it was nothing but an elaborate ploy to get away from her for the weekend (fair enough), but depending on who she told, more men could come snooping.

No, if they'd been smart enough to tempt Colby, Nadia definitely meant a crack in Ivle's defenses, a potential leak— now Colby was gone, perhaps his only potential leak. All his subordinates were blackmailed into submission. He could claim they manufactured libel because he knew their secrets. But Nadia didn't have any secrets; Nadia didn't do anything.

In the past, of course, he'd never had to worry about his wives blabbing whatever it was they thought he might be up to, because his reputation had been so far above reproach. But if Badmonkof was starting to listen to whatever Smutt might have to say, especially after Colby's dastardly idiocy, well, it'd be easy enough….

The political climate Ivle dealt with, as he shuffled between Swiverlia and Mertria, was really quite the same as that torturing Krakoveen in Livonia with generals who favored their own 401K plans over enacting defensive procedures; it was every bit as slithery. Robustly self-serving.

Ivle just had to be careful, that was all. He'd never been this close to ruin before, and that was saying quite a bit because he really wasn't very close to ruin to begin with—

Pity, though, that the divorce had to come along at just the wrong time— or would that actually serve to discredit whatever it was Nadia might inadvertently reveal?

Would she even have anything to inadvertently reveal, in the first place?

Probably not, from what he knew of her.

But that was just the thing, she might not know what she was talking about, but Ivle could never be sure what details of his plans she knew well enough to let slip. There'd been that—incident with the hen charity….

And of course, she could always simply give off some accidental accusation that'd prove coincidentally believable.

But if Ivle simply made Nadia disappear, she'd be missed; he'd shown her off at one too many public functions. No, —but how to get her to stop gossiping? How to isolate her? Make sure she didn't commit multiple faux-pas with every breath she took —without giving her cause to complain later, when he inevitably had to show the world she was still living.

He just needed to keep her away from any of the wheedling politicians who frequented his world— just for a while, until his balancing act between Livonia and Mertria wasn't so crucially levered.

He could just see her, joking with Badmonkof about 'what a crazy thing' her husband had just done recently, while Smutt listened. No, that wouldn't do. And Ivle couldn't really buy Badmonkof believing Nadia was smart enough to manufacture discrediting assertions just to further her own claims when it came to their divorce proceedings.

Whatever shc said, it'd only come out in snippets, obviously undigested, genuine knowledge. It was almost more dangerous that Nadia couldn't connive. She might keep that list of affairs Ivle'd had or— whatever else she used to complain to Jacobsan about him— but if she ever got wind of any political intrigue, that information would be of a different caliber enough to be instantly noticeable.

And Nadia was just the sort of person to look for something she could use against Ivle, if someone offered her money to do so.

—Maybe… he could say it was for her own safety.

That was right— just because they were divorcing didn't mean he didn't still care for her, theoretically.

He'd simply develop an imminent, convenient worry someone might target her. Kidnap her. Or hurt her. Then he could justify keeping her out of society for a while, if he made his precautions look genuine enough. After all, kidnapping was probably how he could interpret whatever methods Smutt'd use to bring her in as a witness, to lend credence to back up Colby's claims.

If it was, after all, Smutt who Ivle had to look out for….

Chapter 11

Evelle Ivle had first met Captain Visen Sfesen the day after she received Mertria's Bonmount Acour, the region's highest national honor. Swiverlian dignitaries had attended the ceremony, of course, as a subtle reminder Mertria was now officially classified as only semi-autonomous, and therefore now completely under the sway of Swiverlia's power.

Visen'd been called into the Swiverlian officers' offices after her acceptance speech. Her own commanding officer had come to tell her, blustering about how she was no doubt destined for promotion, perhaps as high as Swiverlian Federal ranks. Corvan had already been pre-disposed towards optimism that day, at the honor of his team-member being awarded.

But Visen'd actually been called in because Ivle knew she used amphetamines to cement her position as one of Mertria's first ever female SEALs.

He'd first noticed her unnatural quickness the very night for which they were honoring her now.

A Mertrian hospital, just south of the Livonian border, had exploded thanks to insurgents, and she'd been forced to retrieve 10 teammates and countless civilians from the rubble. An unnatural strength and determination. Ivle'd followed up on it. For months. Then finally, a friend of his had found her stash.

Odd, how even horse-pulls stagger the weight allotted each animal according to size, but not the SEALs. Visen was called upon to lift 20% more of her bodyweight than any other man on the team, though even for men, the Veterans' Affairs Department seemed to prefer paying for painful knee operations once the SEALs turned thirty or so.

Ivle had shooed the rest of the Swiverlian officials out of the room that day, like he held some special power to use their private workroom as needed.

"I haven't told anyone, you know," he'd smiled at Visen. "Not yet."

"If you haven't then I assume you don't have any proof." Visen had stared evenly and straight into his eyes. —This'd been before she'd grown tired from life's soullessness.

She wouldn't have thought Ivle had the authority to tell anyone about her amphetamines in the first place; he was well known in Mertria as the cover-boy for civilian defense industry contracts. His accolades, if military, would be entirely honorary— wouldn't they? Visen couldn't be sure, that first time they'd met, if she recognized the unique Swiverlian insignia that seemed to have popped up miraculously on the lapels of Ivle's jacket—

Oh no, he had proof, though. He'd shown her.

"—Don't you know what a danger you'd pose to your teammates, should you inopportunely run out?"

"They're a danger to me if they run out of food or water or sleep."

"Still, I don't think brass would enjoy knowing you used street drugs while working for one of Mertria's most important contingencies, do you?"

They weren't 'street drugs.' They were prescribed. In civilian life they were fine to use, when necessary for the mental handicaps they helped Visen overcome.

So fuck the bastards who wouldn't let her serve her country the best way she knew how. Fuck the assumption it was amphetamines and not her who'd won the Bonmount Acour.

And fuck Ivle's grotesque, needling use of the subjunctive to suggest she was under his control: *'I don't think brass would enjoy knowing…'*

"Are you insinuating there may be a way my superiors don't find out about this?"

Accuse her of drug-use, she'd accuse him of blackmail. Tit for tat.

"That's exactly what I'm insinuating."

"Oh." She hadn't expected that. "Doesn't sound very professional for a military consultant."

Ivle laughed. "Don't play dumb."

Oddly, his smile was almost reassuring, like he'd finally lifted the veil and admitted what no one else was honest enough to own up to. "The SEALs would never take you back if they found out, but I could use your… unique set of skills."

"Would you say the same thing if I were a man?"

It took Ivle a moment to realize what she'd thought he'd implied.

"I meant in a paramilitary capacity. Don't flatter yourself."

Visen actually grinned and leaned forward. "Okay. Would I be payed?"

"Well, your assignment to SEAL team 7 would remain intact, if you accept my offer, so you can continue to receive that pay, but we would also pay for all expenses accrued while working for us, so, play it right, you might not even need a side source of income."

"Who is 'us'?"

"OPSAI. You'd be working under me."

OPSAI was the civilian-lead Task Force charged with stabilizing peace once Mertria'd become one of Swiverlia's semi-autonomous republics.

"You're Swiverlian?"

OPSAI may have been civilian-lead, but the Swiverlians weren't about to allow any of those civilians to be Mertrian; that was standard protocol.

"Yes; I'm Swiverlian. Do I do a Mertrian accent that well? You seem surprised."

Visen'd always been told Ivle was from Mertria.

"If you're Swiverlian why not just use the contingencies Swiverlia assigned for OPSAI?" There'd be no language barrier. "They'd be just as skilled as me, if not more so."

"Yes, but for some jobs they wouldn't have the loyalty you can provide. You understand?"

Dishonorable discharge looked awful bad, when you tried to get back into civilian life. More importantly, Visen was one of the first female SEALs to have won recognition. All the hopes and dreams she would betray, fueling false counterarguments to feminine employment, just because—they'd say—she'd taken the easy way out.

"So. I'd have—"

"More off the radar jobs, and an incentive not to tell. Like I said, I'll even let you keep a desk job with the SEALs."

Visen had hated that desk job. After 36 missions it'd been an insult. Of course, after about two months in, Ivle'd insured all the desk job's responsibilities subtly petered out, and she was left only with the tasks his men set for her, and the threat of dishonorable discharge looming over her forever, should she ever point out to former commanders precisely what the patterns in her reassignment paperwork implied.

Ivle, it seemed, had agents everywhere—even tucked away in the back-storage closets of whatever clerking department determined the fate of SEALs who took on office work.

Visen'd double-checked of course, to ensure he really did work for OPSAI—not just some needling bureaucrat excusing personal interests. Then she'd checked to make sure OPSAI actually was what it claimed to be—but it had all checked out, all the way up Swiverlia's chain of command (which of necessity overtopped Mertria's own). Blackmail really was just the secretive underbelly of their new peace-keeping task force. Not that Mertrian politics had ever been a beacon of black-mail free transparency.

~*~

Now, Visen sat in front of Ivle's desk again, not entirely affable. She was too tired for that by now. OPSAI had turned out to be just like every other shadow government; what the Gestapo had been to the SS; a bureaucratic monstrosity that seemed to have been designed purposefully to butt heads together.

And Visen was far too physically exhausted by now, from rounding up dissidents and political undesirables for OPSAI, to see much difference in her day to day activities and those of the dreaded KGB. Different scale, perhaps. Same control over life and limb. And it all boiled down to this stuffy, imminently civilian contractor, bribed into a Councilor position in Swiverlian government— or whatever it was Ivle nominally did as head of OPSAI— forever smiling and toadying after the gracious thought that someday he could pull a Stalin and take over.

"I want you to look after my wife while I'm away." he'd told Visen to pack her bags for about a week and a half's deployment, with all the standard reconnaissance and security gear, before ushering her into his own private vacation home. Now he sat watching her, analyzing whether it had been a mistake to let such a nonentity see the more intimate details of his life, his double-chin stubbled over his papers like some grumpy frog, internally in tune with the ticking mantel clock behind him. "It'll just be for a few days." Surely Nadia couldn't fuck everything up in just a few days. He could always kill Visen at the end of it all; they both knew that.

"Is this because of the leak?"

"What leak?"

"With— Colby." Visen'd assumed— if Ivle wanted the name of the man Colby'd been with….

—But that had 100% not been her fault.

Visen'd told Colby nothing more than he needed to know for his upcoming mission with the Chevette. She had no idea how he'd managed to de-compartmentalize Ivle's iron-clad assembly line and find precisely the worst person to hand over a floppy disk to— because, frankly, she had no clear understanding that's what he'd managed to do.

But she did know she must've been one of the last Bravos to associate with Colby before whatever mission he'd been on went wrong, and Ivle did have a habit of drawing on subordinates he blamed to help clean up whatever mess he blamed them for, so….

"No, it's— nothing to do with that. It's just your turn to look after her." Ivle grinned.

Visen doubted that. Very much. She'd never heard of anyone else having to guard a Mrs. Ivle before. She would have heard rumors. One of the other subordinates Ivle blackmailed would have told her. There were only about five other women she'd met in Ivle's employ. And she couldn't exactly see Ivle leaving his wife alone with one of the men. Hulking, sexy— everything breast implants were made to seduce.

Of course, subordinates weren't allowed to talk amongst themselves that often, unless they were expendable. Then they had at least five times they could see a fellow worker, before knowing too much, which meant they had to be eliminated.

But that didn't mean they didn't exchange some information. Visen distinctly remembered other Bravos asking her to describe Ivle's wife, when she'd been called to their private home in Swiverlia for debriefing last November.

Surely the other Bravos wouldn't have been as interested, if house duty was an actual thing.

She wondered vaguely if this would be the same wife she'd seen last time.

"Are you sure you're not punishing me for something by taking me off active duty? Because I swear I had nothing to do with Colby's— y'know,"

It wasn't that she minded coming off active duty; she could use the rest. She just feared what it might mean for her ranking in a system it hadn't taken long to realize would never let her go free without a bullet through the brain.

"No, I'm not punishing you." Ivle wasn't used to being questioned by subordinates. But candor seemed to take care of whatever Visen had been searching for.

He couldn't tell if she was under the impression Colby himself had been betrayed.

Something in his eyes accidentally confirmed it had been the other way around, and Ivle could tell for just a split second that Visen realized this was the case, based solely on the way he'd just reacted.

Visen didn't usually think it was professional to pick up on that sort of conversational undercurrent. It wasn't exactly helpful, being able to track things like Colby's attraction to her so minutely; how it first peaked, then stumbled, caught itself up with a haughty over-estimation of its own capacity to hide—all distilled from the ways in which he instigated small talk— especially when no one else was ever willing to verify the sorts of things Visen would notice; 'oh, they're just tired,' they'd say; 'don't worry about it.'

So she usually disregarded nuances, to keep from being intimidated by ulterior motives while everyone else could simply sweep into a room self-assured.

But now, Ivle's uneasiness— an unexpected betrayal might explain the sudden need for additional security, if what Visen guessed was true.

She'd never heard of a Bravo betraying Ivle before, though.

Colby must have introduced some new danger; enough to keep Mrs. Ivle under lock and key?

Or, if Colby had leaked information, Ivle might want to keep Visen off-duty till he could be sure all her information was too outmoded to sell, in case incomplete transmission forced whomever Colby'd been working with—Smutt, Visen supposed—to come find her and offer a deal. As one of the last Bravos to collaborate with Colby, she might be easiest to track.

Course that'd mean Ivle'd be decommissioning other agents as well, surely.

Visen would have asked 'why me?'—why choose her in particular to guard his wife? —bypass all pretense of a rotating schedule— but she supposed it was obvious.

She'd guessed right.

Ivle might not mind a few fucks with a one night stand himself, but he couldn't trust his wife to do the same without accidentally betraying secrets to one of his hulking subordinates, or worse, bringing home some assassin whose real target for the evening was Ivle himself. Having Visen around could guard against both those contingencies, without any threat of seducing Nadia.

"Alright. Any particular duties I should be aware of?"

"Ah. Well. I suppose I should let you know." Ivle fidgeted. "Really it's obvious; you've seen it on the news I'm sure. It's just a very sensitive time right now—and, we've all been warned, as public servants, that attempted kidnappings may force spouses to tell secrets, that sort of thing— or maybe, threatening spouses could be used to take advantage of the situation between Livonia and Mertria; anything. Either way, the insurgents have been making threats. So, I just wanted to take some extra precautions, just to be sure. That's why I'm diverting you in particular, for additional support."

"Got it." Seemed reasonable enough she could believe it, without worrying over whatever additional information had obviously been left out.

"The main thing—just while I'm gone these few days—is to make sure my wife doesn't see anyone, you know, besides the servers, not even manicurists, or specialists, —just put them all off, till I get back. She's just— very gullible; I don't want her being lured anywhere; you understand? That's why, as I say, family friends, whoever it is, just put them off, till I get back. Got it?"

"Yes sir."

"Alright." She seemed unquestioning enough. "Let me show you the house."

~*~

Swimming pool.
Garage—

There was a handheld buzzer to stick in your car for the door to open remotely, and two buttons on the garage's left wall labelled 'port 1' and 'port 2'.

Visen wouldn't be using the car though. The Ivles had all their groceries delivered.

Main hall.

Atrium.

Security cameras.

Security guard's gatehouse, by the gate which spanned across a gravel drive they only ever opened up for parties. The gatehouse came complete with the security guard named Wheeler, who commanded a task force of three, in charge of securing the grounds. Ivle provided a phone number to the gate house in case Visen ever needed back up.

Following round to the other side of the mansion, there was an indoor sauna. Ferns. Yellow striped towels. Ivle even showed Visen how to work the jacuzzi. Could be a relaxing assignment for once. The indoor pool overlooked a private cliff face, with a dock-house by a beach where Ivle stored his yacht when in season.

Precipice looked quite unscalable, so one could feel secure looking out over the waves while enjoying the comforts of a full-service bar.

Full service in that it contained every type of alcohol under the sun. Ivle didn't trust bartenders. He only hired a cook—who kept to her own separate quarters and the kitchen—and landscaping people, who came in twice a month to blow leaf-blowers indeterminately against the sharp confines of perfectly manicured grass.

He showed Visen the key to his main office, right before putting it in his pocket, where it would remain for the duration of his absence. But their WiFi router was in that room, so if anything went wrong, she needed to call him.

Upstairs, there were several bathtubs and four-poster beds.

"Nadia?" Ivle called out, looking round.

Nadia was slumped three rooms away, in front of a television blaring mid-day soap operas, fully ensconced in a cube stacking game on her phone. At the sound of approaching husband, though, she straightened up instantly and went to go rearrange the nearest vase full of cattails and subulates, as though perpetually in the process of charming her home with effortless grace— and ferns which may at one point have not been synthetic.

"Nadia?"

She looked up from where she'd been siphoning two-inch nails through fake foliage. Evelle was in slightly rumpled business slacks, and looking preoccupied, while behind him Captain Visen stood with her hands behind her back, packing enough spare Kevlar to dismantle a bomb.

Just what were they playing at?

"I'm gonna be gone for a little while, alright? Starting this evening. In the meantime, this lady's gonna take care of you and make sure everything's okay, alright?"

Evelle'd forgotten they'd met before, hadn't he?

Nadia'd secn the way he looked at Visen last time; it was the same way he was looking at her now—as though perpetually gauging whether his wife would detract from impressions he was fit to command.

Was this Evelle trying to be clever?

Some prelude to offers of a threesome?

Evelle never hired guards. Not for Nadia. Honestly, all Evelle ever did with Nadia was share sexual escapades.

"You're going away?"

"Yup." That was the one bit of conversation they'd shared over dinner last night. He distinctly remembered her responding, "oh, okay."

Turns out he could tell her he was off to nuke Russia and she'd still say the same thing.

Of course, 'uh huh?', 'yeah,' and 'oh cool,' had been about the sum extent of Nadia's vocabulary even back when they'd first started dating, but back then it'd been a bit more exciting to have such a pretty, wealthy face willing to take in whatever he chatted about while giving great fellatio. Come to think of it, he'd known even then she had nothing between the ears with which to process what he said.

"Where are you going?"

Visen's eyes flicked between the two of them. Had he not told her he was leaving?

"Well." Ivle sat beside his wife, looking cramped. "You remember all that fuss about how one country wanted to get even with another country, so they had that security breach?"

"Yeah."

"Well I've got to go fix that, only it's gotten a bit more involved than usual, so I want Lieutenant Visen here to stay with you in case you need anything, to make sure you feel safe."

Nadia looked back over at Visen, with what would have been distrust, had a lifetime of habit not smoothed all wrinkle-inducing emotion from her face.

"Okay…?"

"Right." Ivle didn't want to mention in front of Visen they'd been arguing recently. "Just wanted you to, y'know, know, that I care about you, so you can be sure: there's nothing to worry about. There might be some security precautions, but they're all here only just in case, just till I get back, so, there's nothing to worry about,"

There. That should freak her out enough. He explained it with all the tact of convincing a toddler it was time for bed, then pat her comfortingly on the thigh in the same motion with which he propelled himself towards exiting the room, hoping to avoid giving Nadia some sort of in, in front of Visen, by which to start arguing again.

"So, you're just leaving me here with Bravo 2?"

"Uh-huh, yeah," Ivle tried to gloss over the fact Nadia knew Visen's confidential code-name.

"But you'll still keep communicating with her the entire time while you're gone."

"Yeah, make sure you're safe,"

"While I'm stuck in this house and can't leave."

"Uh-huh, yeah; it'll just be for about a week,"

"But you'll be communicating with her like, every day, as usual."

"Uh, uh-huh, yeah, as needed."

"Uh-huh." She let them almost leave the room. Ivle thought he'd done a pretty good job getting his one female Bravo settled in without Na— "So what's she got that I haven't got, anyway?"

—Ap! *There it was.* See, this was precisely what Ivle didn't want; Nadia voicing inappropriate assumptions. And it was pretty disastrously obvious from the way she plucked self-consciously at her plunging neckline that she wasn't just referring to Visen's finer-tuned capacities when it came to self-defense.

Nadia knew they'd been 'talking' in Ivle's office. The CCTV cameras had picked them up going in together.

He tried to laugh it off lovingly, "I'll see you real soon—"

"No, no, come on. What's she got that I haven't?"

"Nothing," Visen straightened from where she'd slouched against the doorway, looking genuinely confused, but also a little bit like she'd finally caught on to Nadia's suspicions they were fucking.

"Uh-huh," Ivle's wife could exude a very particular quality all of her own— it was actually quite a remarkable ability: she'd done nothing but undulate her neck back an inch or two sideways, but it accentuated the breath leaving her larynx in just the right way to imbue it with its own peculiar capacity to communicate simultaneously both slightly disinterested disappointment and disdain.

Ok, so maybe this assignment wasn't going to be any less stressful than Visen's other duties.

Nadia went back to over-scrutinizing ferns.

"I told her I was going out of town yesterday," Ivle muttered on their way back to the elevator.

"How long does this assignment last?" Visen had almost called it a 'deployment.'

"Ten days, tops."

Ivle was just going back to Jolinta to make sure Smutt hadn't been making libelous accusations about him (and to make some libelous accusations of his own, about Smutt).

He went to collect a few briefcases one of his Livonian lawyers had just brought down for him.

"Do I have anything in particular I ought to look out for?" Visen stood beside him, at ease, but only by official military definitions. "Breaking and entry? Poison?"

"No, it wouldn't be an execution; not on her at any rate." Just the soldier guarding her, probably.

"So, extortion?"

Ivle feathered his hands in opposite directions as if to say, 'who's to know?' "Just make sure she doesn't talk to anybody. Tell my lawyers I'll be back in a few days, if they drop by."

"Alright."

"And by— I mean, *anybody*. Don't let her talk to the lawyers, not to telemarketers, not the lawns-crew. Don't let anybody in the house. Don't let her chat on the landline; she could be making plans. I don't want her to get worried, but I don't know who we can trust at this point, so, just, you know, for her sake, we gotta shut it all down. It's easier. And that way, I don't have to disturb her, by telling her how serious this all is. It's just— blanket— we shut it all down."

He'd put a lock on Nadia's phone as well, for those ten days, just in case. She'd once emailed a gossip column and told them all about an orgy he'd hosted. Well, no more. She could still access websites from the phone, but she couldn't text, email, or comment on any social media platforms while he was away. So he wouldn't come home and find paparazzi like last time. Official search warrants Ivle could handle; paparazzi could find anything. "I'll reinstate everything once I get back, of course; I'm just worried. That's partially why you're here. You'll be able to help if she needs anything. But make sure, you know, she doesn't start talking to anybody in the meantime, get in some nice little chat that ends in her agreeing to meet passerbys in the potting shed, you know what I mean? We're just— in lock down mode for now, safe house style, yeah? Just till I return."

Who, exactly, among Nadia's friends, did Ivle suspect was going to kidnap her for insurgents?

"Now, your bedroom's on the fourth floor, right above Nadia's. You're allowed to use the phone, of course; there's one in your room. And I've opened a surveillance panel so you can keep an eye on her and swing down if you need to intervene; it's got a—pulley."

'Surveillance panel' apparently meant a panel one took out of the floor to gain access to lower rooms via the ceiling.

"Oh."

Not creepy at all.

"I've never seen one of those before."

How many of these were dotted through the house? And why had they ever been installed?

"Swiverlian precautions." Ivle smiled sweetly.

Bit paranoid for a civilian contractor, no?

Even if he was OPSAI-coordinator.

It began to dawn on Visen that Ivle must be remarkably higher up in the official rankings of Swiverlian politics than he'd ever let on before.

"Alright," he popped closed the door to a subsidiary study. "That should be everything. Oh, TV remote."

"Thanks."

"And don't—tell her how seriously we're taking these precautions, right? I don't want her worried. Just keep it light and breezy. I mean, obviously, she's not the brightest—maybe— but—she is my wife, and I want to come back to find her here, you know what I mean?"

"Yeah."

The look in his eyes promised he shared the same basic possessiveness for the Bentley that pulled up now, but it seemed meant to be understood by Visen as a cheeky 'just-between-us-two' sort of look, as though promising 'we have great sex, because our marriage is ideal, and I am perfect.'

It was always odd when people forgot Visen wasn't a man. She took it as a compliment —they'd finally seen past her physical form —but at the same time, such a disturbing window into reality…. That you could mean nothing personal by assumptions akin to owning another person. It wasn't just Visen misinterpreting, by taking it too personally, not quite.

"I have a feeling," Ivle leaned closer, for stricter confidence, "she may be cheating on me with someone. I don't believe that's acceptable behavior; it's not something I like in a wife, but, it could put her in danger. I mean, this is why that sort of behavior isn't allowed, by any— rational— system. She just, doesn't—she just lacks the basic perceptiveness, you know? So, I want her under lock and key, you understand?"

"Yes sir."

"Just don't let her go out to lunch with strange men, okay?" parting narcissism required he pull a joke as he rolled his bags out to the Bentley. Visen nodded, waved. Ivle looked back one last time, as his car swept out of sight, for the final acknowledgment of a dipped chin from where Visen splayed robotically into a post beside the front door.

Honestly, as of now, Visen was probably the best asset Ivle had. She was hulking enough to be bodyguard, yet Ivle had the satisfaction of knowing she looked nothing like the gardeners whose first day on the grounds corresponded almost exactly to the day Nadia decided to take up nude sunbathing.

Now if only he could convince Badmonkof whatever warnings Smutt might be spouting were absolute tripe.

Chapter 12

Visen stood looking like she'd just slammed her face into a wall, until the gates closed behind her boss' Bentley with a hollow, soulful clanging. Well, standing here was superfluous. They already had a guard at the front entryway.

She took the small rucksack she'd brought with her back up to the room Ivle'd assigned her instead. It looked so out of place amid the plushy purple couch cushions. This'd certainly be different from her regular assignments, boring, probably.

Visen peered a half inch down through the hole in her floor. She could see the chandelier in Nadia's room. Felt like she was violating her privacy—she turned on the TV instead.

Oh.

It was helpfully wired to present automatically visuals from CCTV footage for every single room in the house, apparently—in a continuous reel, if you kept it on Channel 2.

So that's why Ivle'd been sure to hand her the remote.

She left the TV on in the background, flickering through its silent images of an eerily lifeless baroque architecture, and went to call down to the guard in his metallic bull pen by the gate, to let him know she had a second set of eyes on the same surveillance feed she'd noticed he watched, and to ask, since this was so, if they could arrange alternating shifts when it came to their sleep schedules.

Turns out, they could. She'd be getting 8 hours of sleep for the first time in her adult life. Nice perk.

She settled into a window seat in her room which overlooked a back lawn and started reading the novel she'd bought on purpose for the occasion.

Visen was a slow reader; she had no doubt it'd take her about 5 days to complete *Moby Dick*. Especially when she was obliged to skim the 72 surveillance feeds that cycled through her television's screen—

But that duty, now, would only begin at eight PM, when the evening guard was due to switch places with his replacement.

Of course, on second thought, a guard down by the gates wouldn't be able to run up here in time, if Nadia's room itself were infiltrated. Visen began flickering her attention between *Moby Dick* and the surveillance monitor ahead of schedule, just in case.

About thirty minutes in, she realized Nadia hadn't moved. She was just sitting there, playing that cube stacking game on her phone.

It really would be so much easier to keep visuals on her if they simply sat in the same room together.

Visen went downstairs and knocked on the open door.

"Ms. Ivle? Your husband just left. Do you mind if I come in?"

Nadia straightened, nonplussed, "no. Do you need something?"

"No. But if I stay in here with you, it'll be easier to ensure your safety. Would you be comfortable with that?"

"S'fine. Am I in danger?" She watched Visen sit.

"Ah, no I don't think so, not really. Your husband's just being extra cautious."

"Oh. Okay."

Surely, she'd noticed the new sense of urgency sweeping through Mertria's threats against Livonia? The comings and goings at night—hadn't Colby mentioned attending secretive cabinet meetings at Ivle's?

From the blank lack of fear in Nadia's vocalization, it sounded like she'd never even heard of Livonia.

"What's he being cautious for?"

Ah. So, that was a "no," then: she had not noticed politicians were abnormally worried.

"So, it's just in case anyone wants to apply pressure, to try to manipulate the negotiations between Livonia and Mertria going on right now."

"Oh. So like kidnapping." Now they were on the same page.

"Yeah, or just, you know, any sort of threatening, really. So, I'll just be over here reading, alright? You let me know if you need anything."

"Okay."

Of course, it's absolutely unpleasant to have a perfect stranger just sitting there, when you're so used to being left alone. Nadia's need to be hospitable kept distracting her from sinking back into the comfort of being consumed by her own thoughts. It was impossible to relax into fully being oneself when another person was in the room.

"You want some fruit?" she finally caved. "Here, let me get you some fruit." Every day, the chef left her a huge punch-bowl full of fruit to pick through. It was part of her juice cleanse. She shuffled two ladles' worth of honeydew, strawberries, and pineapple onto one of the paper plates stacked habitually by her crystal bowl's side, to ease the necessity of grazing throughout the day.

"Oh; thank you." Visen couldn't read and balance a fruit plate at the same time.

I mean, she could try, but there were cameras in every room and her boss would most likely be reviewing the surveillance reels.

"Do you like it?"

"Mm, yes it's very good, thank you," everything tasted like lemon juice.

"It's supposed to be good for your complexion,"

"Oh."

Silence.

"What are you reading?"

"Moby Dick,"

"Oh, I've heard of that. It's about whales isn't it?"

"Yeah; it's pretty good."

~*~

Ivle, meanwhile, was relaxing in the back of his chauffeured car, safe in the knowledge Visen would put a stop to any 'friendly chats' with his wife as he travelled steadily towards the Mertrian capitol.

He was still going to divorce Nadia as soon as this was all over; he just had to keep her quiet for the time being, didn't want her singing his condemnations to the hills.

Meanwhile: to convince Badmonkof Colby had been ordered to give Smutt information that was obviously fabricated to discredit Ivle—possibly, by the Livonians—?

Ivle's original plan had been to convince Mertria that Livonia had planted plans implying nuclear warheads in amongst Mertria's databases, to give themselves an excuse for invasion—thereby giving Mertria an excuse to invade Livonia.

He now had two options. He could either pretend to be working for Livonia himself, in which case, the temptation necessary to spur Mertria to war would still be supplied, to Ivle's detriment, or, he could claim Colby had been working for Livonia, in a two pronged approach: not only tasked with planting fodder for a war between the two Republics, but also serving to discredit the only man who stood as mediator between Livonia,

Mertria, and utter chaos (Ivle himself). Ivle liked that option better.

The plan practically wrote itself. He could even incorporate Smutt's offer to bribe Colby (thank god for Jacobsan and his fine ears), as proof Smutt was working for Livonia, thereby discrediting his potential discrediter before the latter had time to discredit Ivle.

Unfortunately, the Mertrian President was still smarting over the fact Ivle'd forced him to take aid from the very enemy perpetually about to invade his country—

Of course he was happy to hear Smutt's suspicions Ivle was in fact a Livonian agent, caught red-handed planting proofs of nonexistent nukes.

What Ivle had to do now was backpedal.

Because if Mertria didn't come crawling to Swiverlia for help this time round—put off by Ivle's seemingly less than altruistic meddling, as Swiverlia's unofficial representative—it might start a new trend. Certainly, wouldn't help Swiverlia's hopes for expansion, were the Autonomous Republics to realize they were being played against one another.

Luckily, even as only an unofficial representative of Swiverlia, Ivle still had enough authority Badmonkof felt obligated to grant him an audience.

He started right in.

"You think I told Colby to plant nuclear— whatever—to frame Mertria and give Livonia a chance to invade; that's what Smutt's told you, hasn't he?"

Ivle had agents with their ears to the ground in all Semi-Autonomous Republics. He knew all the local gossip—but he could have told you himself Smutt had gotten to Badmonkof first, judging solely by the way everyone in the office was giving him stink-eye.

"But it wasn't on my authority that Colby did this; think about it; why would I want to destroy a peace I had just brokered? Colby acted alone, without my knowledge, for Livonia, then claimed I was the one who put him up to it. His objective wasn't to plant proof of some random nuclear device amongst your arsenals; it was to incriminate me,"

"Why?" Badmonkof was, unfortunately, not taking kindly to Ivle's backpedaling. He fingered the floppy disk Smutt had brought him defensively.

"So next time confrontation sparks off between Mertria and Livonia, I won't be there to bring you and Krakoveen together because you won't trust me anymore. And we both know, if Livonia fights, they will win. See how much more sense it makes for them to be trying to get me out of the way?"

"But…" Badmonkof had meant 'why would your subordinate plant insinuations we have a secret nuclear armory, just to discredit you?'

"He was paid; my lawyer Jacobsan is prepared to testify that he overheard—"

"I don't trust your lawyers—"

"Then I'm sure my door guard will corroborate!"

Wheeler was always safe to use as a loyal witness. He actually believed in Ivle enough to want to take an active part in furthering the peace-ensuring aims of OPSAI. "He heard Smutt promise Colby large sums of money should Colby find anything incriminating against me to show him. That gave Livonia the in they needed—"

"So you're saying Smutt's working for Livonia?"

"Well, I have proof he's definitely responsible for providing a motive to fabricate the most damning evidence possible against me," Ivle handed over print outs of the transaction history between Colby and Smutt's personal bank account.

Smutt had paid half the reward he'd promised—to be topped up once Colby actually delivered his information—into a secret offshore account Colby kept.

But Ivle knew all about Colby's secret offshore account because he was the one who had set it up for him.

"That doesn't prove anything. He put out feelers for incriminating evidence, and he found it."

Badmonkof wasn't taking kindly to Ivle's warnings about Smutt either. He found it a bit suspicious Ivle could incriminate the one cabinet member clever enough to incriminate Ivle. "There's no connection between Smutt and Livonia; if he did bribe Colby out of his own funds he was acting in good faith! I can personally vouch for him!"

That was the problem with smaller governments. Bunch of good old boys…. Ok, Ivle could play that game too.

"He doesn't have to have connections to Livonia. Smutt obviously dislikes me; he's disliked me from the start; I'm saying Livonians used the opportunity he unknowingly provided. He's gunning to replace me as your consultant; he's been gunning to replace me since the beginning; probably doesn't trust Swiverlians."

"Really? Would he be so petty?"

"Wars are won and lost over petty things. Aren't they? Y'know, that's the worst of it. I like Smutt. I truly believe he truly believes I'm not the best for this job. He's a patriot, that's what's really been hard for me, and patriots will do all sorts of things to keep their country safe; he's just barking up the wrong tree. Look; you want proof? Here. These floppies are compatible with my defensive systems. Put it in. I'm assuming that's the floppy Smutt's given you, from Colby?" Badmonkof had taken it out when he saw Ivle coming to confront him with it. "Go on, put it in your computer. Here, I'll put it in for you; better yet, let's put it in the actual main drive. I know how to work these things; I'll prove I had nothing to do with this. Right now."

Fifty minutes later they were in a highly secured training compound, in fact, the very highly secured training compound Colby ought to have brought the floppy disk to in the first place. Crassburger was in attendance, glaring daggers at Ivle for weaseling his way out of any accountability, because he knew he himself couldn't come forward to back up Smutt's claims without a few overly-opportune car crashes in his past being brought up as counter-incentive.

"Now, we run the program, see?" Ivle put the floppy disk in.

"Like so." Might as well download that incriminating evidence of a nonexistent nuclear reactor now while he was at it, just in case he ever did get a chance to show Livonia. "Now, here, the code appears, see? A time stamp, right here. Now, this granular texture—see? That shows there's a physical copy of this floppy on microfilm, somewhere, from which this floppy was made.

"Now, the reason this is important. Say you uploaded this in order to plant the impression that Mertria had access to warheads that don't actually exist. Just say. Like, I don't know what this is exactly but, unless you can memorize this entire—whatever it is, you're gonna wanna make sure you have a record of what you originally put into the Mertrian system, aren't you?"

"Why?"

"Well—say someone comes along and says 'oh my God! Mertria has 7 nuclear missiles. And you stop and think 'wait, no, I only uploaded proof they have two nuclear missiles'—"

"I think this is just one—"

"Doesn't matter—" Ivle'd made damn sure his hypotheticals didn't actually match up in any way with the specifics of a floppy disk about which he was claiming absolutely no knowledge.

"What I'm saying, is that you need to keep tabs on the original, to make sure no one else is trying to take advantage of the situation, right? This is called Contractor's Liability where I come from, it's very important; you keep an original of all documents otherwise someone'll come back and say, 'hey, the original plans you quoted your estimate on included a jacuzzi' and you'd be like 'no, that didn't include a jacuzzi' and they'd have doctored it to look like you'd made them agree to build you a jacuzzi for 395. Does that make sense?"

"Well I don't really see—" Badmonkof didn't appreciate the references to a jacuzzi.

"What I'm saying is whoever made this will have kept a hard copy that isn't connected to my central servers,"

"Why couldn't they just access the file again—"

"Because you'd see it when they tried to access; that's— literally the entire safety protocol behind the system we've just installed,"

"What if you converted it to a different file type and uploaded it to a different type of comput—"

"No remember that's the entire joy of our defensive system; these files can't be converted without alerting your system; you'd still see—so, if someone wanted to use this information against you, they would, need access to it, wouldn't you say that's a fair assumption? Right. So. How do they do that?"

"With a—"

"With a hard copy, that's right. A hardcopy to reference and the hard copy that's needed to boot up the main frame to make copies of it editable, in case they want to make changes. Alright?" The copy otherwise known as a 'mother copy,' which Ivle, fortunately, hadn't fully explained to Badmonkof when he'd sold it as part of his defense-network package to the Mertrians. Always good to keep something back for later. Now he could emphasize how many extraneous precautions ensured his networks were normally impenetrable. "So. Whoever has that hard copy, must be whoever put Colby up to this. We just have to find whoever has that hard copy."

"Okay."

"Which should be fairly easy. Microfilm—the stuff it's you know, printed on originally, that stuff has specific chemical components we can trace down partially by analyzing the granulation you can see on your screen here, you see that? That's a particular chemical fingerprint; we can trace that, alright?"

"And you'd—help with—?"

"Of course. See, this is why I'm so worried; this is as much an offense against Swiverlia as it is against Mertria. Mertria, you remember, might not even be the final target; they may be trying to sabotage Swiverlian relations as much as Mertrian and Livonian. And that's—now, that's where I come in and I want you to do something for me, okay?" he could see the light of trust creeping back into Badmonkof's eyes. He needed that. "I want you to send your men round, to my house. I will give them full access to every single section of that house. Every single section of all three of my houses. My bank accounts. My secret files, top secret data entry systems," (not the ones that connected him to

Swiverlian high command; they didn't need to know about those ones). "Crassburger, can you think of anything else?"

"We could run a system wide check on you to see where else you keep paperwork."

"Perfect, do that. Do that." Ivle was the one who'd made the system they were going to use to check up on him—

Although, he realized, that would mean they'd discover his additional, mildly secret Mertrian vacation home— the one with Nadia in it. God dammit. Stupid Crassburger. He just had to hope Visen could keep Nadia locked away while Badmonkof's men perused paperwork. Whatever, house was so big Nadia probably wouldn't even notice.

"I mean I don't think we have the manpower to do all that—"

"No. But I do. Now, I want you to know that you can trust me. We're going to go over every one of my houses. Step by step."

"No, no I really don't think that's necessary—"

"No, I insist,"

"He'll just hide it somewhere—"

"What'd you say?"

"I said—never mind—" Poor Crassburger.

"Yeah no, no, that's a good point, you could just hide it somewhere we don't find."

"Ok. Send in your best. Your special ops teams. The ones who know everything about how to find secret documents. Your secret service. You get your guys. I'll get Swiverlia's guys. If they can't find it; it's not there."

"Mmmm…" Badmonkof had had an incident a few years back where he'd been hoarding government bonds in a very clever secret hidey-hole behind his mantel piece, and even so those secret service bastards'd found it.

Ivle was counting on his recollections of that horrible evening to convince him such thoroughness was possible.

"Well…"

"Because I want to prove to you, that you can trust me."

Chapter 13

"Ok," Nadia eventually stopped playing her block-matching game. "I'm gonna go to the Solarium. Do you need to sit in there with me too?"

"No, I can wait outside," the Solarium only had one entry, and the windows were screened off by stucco and reinforced glass warbling. Visen'd hear if anyone tried to break in.

There was also another flat-screen TV just outside, with which she could check Channel 2.

Convenient.

Why did Ivle even need her here if he had enough state-of-the-art security to fend off an invasion?

The only thing Visen'd done so far was answer the phone when a family friend called, to tell her Nadia wouldn't be able to go golfing that Saturday. Surely Nadia could be entrusted with that?

Visen began to suspect she'd only been hired because her voice never modulated into eager solicitudes, so she made the perfect bitch to keep well-wishers at bay—*great.*

It was just her mind had other things to do besides focus on how each word fell on others, which, after all, she could never fully expect to control; when politicians spoke with no concern other than veracity and usefulness, it was authority. When her comrades in arms did it, it showed they viewed those they addressed with the equality that comes from a shared purpose. When Visen did it, a society habituated to coddling from those who shared her gender saw it as discourteous—when, in truth, it was simply the flat-lining of all emotion that comes with depression.

Ivle had guards; the guards had explained how easy it was to set off an alarm, or, if need be, a secret signal to the nearest police station. Why was Visen—? To scare Nadia away from talking to the guards?

Why such a gilded penitentiary?

They even rang a bell to let staff know dinner was served at 6. Who ate dinner at 6?

It turned out Visen was the only crew member allowed in the royalty-worthy dining hall. Everyone else ate in the kitchen. It was like Ivle was trying to foster resentment —though, Visen supposed, it was conceivable —if this was what Ivle'd known his whole life— that he actually believed the staff were being friendly, not professional, whenever they smiled and greeted him back.

Nadia'd worn a dress to dinner out of habit. She'd also re-perfected her nails (one had come unglued a bit in the Solarium while she was doing her daily gymnastics routine).

She was pretty sure Visen was wearing the exact same clothes she'd seen her wear the only other time she'd actually seen her in person, last December. It looked like she'd never changed out of them.

They ate cucumber soup together in silence.

"Hey, look at these earrings Evelle just got me," Nadia pivoted to model them for Visen. "They're diamond!"

"Very nice," Visen couldn't really see them; the table was way too long to carry on a normal conversation.

She didn't know what else to say. She didn't really do earrings.

Nadia figured she didn't do earrings. But she looked like she could be interested in diamonds. Didn't Evelle do a lot of diamond runs? Trying to avoid artificial monopolization, stuff like that?

"Do you want some?"

"Sorry?"

"Some earrings."

Nadia usually made conversation by trying on various accoutrements with her friends and commenting on which suited who best. It was how they spent shopping trips. "I know a nice little shop down near the village where Evelle gets his,"

"Oh, no, that's okay," Visen didn't know whether to say thank you or not. She didn't want to look like she'd assumed Nadia was offering a gift; what if she just didn't realize anyone on security detail would never be rich enough to flippantly purchase diamond earrings within their natural lifespan? "It wouldn't look good with my complexion,"

"Oh, okay, yeah."

Oh gawd. How long was this lady going to be staying here? 10 days? (Nadia'd been watching Ivle's retreat to the stairwell when he told Visen 'ten days tops' on Channel 2's live feed).

They finished their cucumber soup in silence. That was all they were having for dinner. "Do you want some sherry?" That's what Ivle always offered guests after dinner.

"Oh. Yes please." Carbs. Visen needed carbs. No wonder this lady couldn't think straight, she survived on cucumbers. Did all the other security guards survive on cucumbers too? This was bad. This was very bad.

"We can go into the drawing room,"

"Ok," Visen's stomach started growling.

"Do you go in for skin care?"

"Ah not usually,"

"Oh."

Nadia did make a gracious host, shepherding Visen to the nearest sofa and nimbly handing over one of the sherries she poured. She just couldn't find a topic Visen wanted to talk about.

"So, what is it you do exactly?"

"I'm a courier, mainly, for your husband,"

"Aw, fancy a courier guarding me," Two sips of sherry were really all it took to make Nadia tipsy. "You're not gonna serve me divorce papers are you?"

"I don't—think those are usually 'served,' are they?"

"Oh, yeah. Heh."

Both finished their first glass of alcohol out of sheer awkwardness.

Second Sherry time! This was how Nadia hung out with friends once it hit 7 pm.

"I remember when Ivle tried to serve me with divorce papers the first time—hah! that was a hoot!"

Flashback: Ivle huff-marching after her, flapping a now thoroughly disorganized bundle of legal documents over his head storming: "You have to sign these! You have to sign at least one!"

She would not sign it!

"Ivle tried to divorce you?"

"Yeah, but I wouldn't let him. I told him if he divorced me, I'd tell Badmonkof all about how he planted that nuke to keep Livonia and Mertria scared, or—"

"Sorry; he planted a what now?"

"Oh no no no sorry not like an actual bomb, sorry—you know, like that blueprint on Mertria's servers? For Livonia to find."

Visen did not know.

"Like—you know; that nuclear reactor thing? —But it kinda like, obviously implied, if they kept a nuclear reactor secret—"

Visen's 'Uh…' slowly morphed into an 'Oh.'

"Sorry, when was this?"

Oh yay! Nadia'd found something Visen was interested in!

"Oh, this was like about a month ago now, but he pesters. I told Jacobsan—that's our lawyer—all about the nuke thing though and he was like yes that's definitely grounds for divorce, so don't expect upheaval too soon; I'm thinking if I have grounds for divorce Evelle's grounds for divorce are sort of cancelled out, you know what I mean?"

"Wait the—sorry, the planting a nuke thing was a month ago? Or the divorce bit?"

"Oh, the nuke was only like a few days ago; that's new; it was on the news—didn't you—like —You were a part of that, weren't you? With the—like you gave them that thing that enabled them to make sure Livonia could see it?"

Nadia read Ivle's texts sometimes. She'd begun reading them a lot more when she'd begun to suspect he had a nuclear power plant he was erroneously dotting around models of the Mertrian countryside. And the secret, coded vocabulary really wasn't that hard to crack: this was Bravo 2; 'package USB' meant 'bomb'….

"It was that thing with the Mertrian data breach? I heard him call you on the phone about it. Well, I mean, he said he was calling Colby, but that means he was calling you too right? Like I know he always does y'all in pairs; he called you right?" It wasn't an accusation— she was too tipsy for that— it was excitement at being right.

"Ah…" Visen realized her jaw had dropped an inch.

"And then you were the one to take that little USB thing he had out for Bravo 3 to take?"

Silence meant yes!

"Yeah that was the little thing that decrypted Mertrian messages for Livonia; Venro told me; he's the one who set it up; he's very nice, Venro."

"Oh."

No wonder Ivle didn't want her talking to anyone.

"So, a USB?"

Like the one Visen had delivered to Max? The Aplidex….

"Yeah, it's this fancy new type of design that fits in with the new defense systems they're building; you have this primary 'mother' copy you leave at home and then you can just plug that in to see when all the daughter copies have been accessed or delete them; it's really handy," Nadia'd listened to Ivle's sales pitch at least five times over dinner. She'd remembered it wrong, but she'd gotten the gist of it.

"And that was last week?" Timing did fit.

"Yeah but the divorce thing was earlier, like that's been going on for months now, but oh my God you shoulda seen him the first time he tried to get me to sign papers; like, he stormed in all fumey too—he gets like that sometimes, fumey."

Somehow it seemed impossible to picture Ivle ever getting 'fumey.' That was precisely his claim to fame: he never got flustered; that's what everyone found so frightening about him.

"No, I'm serious!" Nadia must've seen the disbelief on Visen's face. "It was so awkward too," she scooted forward to underscore the hint of an invitation to take interest in her voice, "'cause right—like literally right when I was threatening to tell Badmonkof about the bomb thing —Jacobsan, that's our lawyer; he actually walked in, like Jacobsan actually walked in. Like he's our friend we do golf together too,"

Oh, that must've been the husband of the lady who'd called earlier—

"And so like he *heard*, but of course now he's on Ivle's side 'cause he caught me halfway through my rant—but that's only because he didn't see how Ivle was going off on me first! Because of course as soon as anyone comes in, he's all like 'ooh I'm Mr. Business as usual nothing flappable about me.' But oh my God you should see him when he's like, when he's not like that it's so funny; he like, storms in like he's like all fumey, he's like rawr rawr rawr rawr rawr rawr!"

Oh, that was beautiful. Something so cathartic about seeing Ivle conceptualized as a dinosaur.

Of course, as soon as Nadia noticed she'd got Visen grinning, she lost her train of thought for a bit. Damn self-consciousness— being so distracting—Visen could tell she faltered.

O-oh, this was all to get attention, wasn't it? The crazy stories, the—of course! She'd been trying to find something that interested Visen since dinner!

If Ivle really was off planting insinuations of nukes, it made taking a few amphetamines to better serve one's country look comparatively tame. The only way Ivle could possibly not worry Nadia would supply Visen with counter blackmail—would be if this was all bullshit to begin with.

Turned out it was really funny bullshit though.

Apparently, there were orgies… stolen Bengal tigers, combinations of orgies and stolen Bengal tigers—Visen was pretty sure Mertrian muckrakers had debunked that one— an Austrian diamond that gave Nadia rashes from radiation—

"Radiation?"

"Yeah. From the actual nuke they never told anyone about,"

Jesus Christ what was happening?

This was only their first conversation and Nadia'd already spilled enough slander to get Ivle executed in every country five times over.

Who cared if it was true or not? Swiverlia's secret police wouldn't; they'd just shoot and ask questions later.

And if Ivle had anything to do with negotiating peace treaties— Nadia could let loose enough gossip to start Armageddon.

"You know, if I didn't know any better, I'd say he put you here to just straight up kill me, like—I swear," (3rd sherry).

"No no I promise I wasn't debriefed on plans to kill anyone,"

"Eh, he probably thinks I'll just drive you to it naturally. —You want some more fruit?"

Oh. She had a fruit bowl in here as well.

"Here, lemme get you some fruit," she refilled her own paper plate too, matter-of-factly.

"Thank you." Now Visen was stuck eating cantaloupe again. To be fair, though, this was the first fruit she'd had in ages.

"So," Nadia settled back in, "there was this other time; he'd just rigged the local elections…"

Chapter 14

Sadly, by the third day, playing bodyguard to Nadia had gotten super awkward.

They simply had absolutely nothing in common. Visen'd taken to trailing after her while she did her skin care routine, which lasted until around noon. Then she'd go into the Solarium and hold her breath in the pool for as long as possible, as a meditative exercise to relax facial muscles, letting bubbles slowly drift to the surface while Visen sat reading Moby Dick pretending not to be rigidly terrified she'd just drowned.

After the bubbles, came lying in a face mask, soaking up sun.

On the first day, Visen'd checked the face mask's multiple tubes of ingredients, to make sure none of the chemicals had been tampered with. Now she just sat back and read, though it felt rude just sitting there when Nadia was so obviously inclined to worry about whether she was comfortable or not.

Temperature-wise:

"Is the room hot enough for you?"

"Oh yes, thank you,"

"I can turn it up if you want,"

"No that's okay,"

…Foodwise: "you know, if you ever get sick of the cucumber soup, cook can order out for any ingredients you want," —ah-hah!

Now that actually was something Visen could want.

"Do you have any bacon?" Bacon was healthy, right? Low carb.

"I can check with the kitchen,"

They had prosciutto. It came out draped over wedges of cantaloupe, but that was fine. It was the first meat Visen'd had in two days. She offered to let Nadia eat the cantaloupe.

"Can't," she pointed to the mask of acai berries and guacamole covering her face.

"Okay."

Visen looked it up: Cantaloupe had 65 calories per slice. It felt so long since she'd eaten 1200 calories a day. She devoured the cantaloupe too.

After facemasks it was time to poof up Nadia's hair with enough setting spray to single-handedly destroy the ozone. That took about 45 minutes. By then, Visen had finally tired of pretending constantly interrupted forays into Melville's descriptions of whale blubber were actually more interesting than the woman sitting in front of her.

"So, you do swimming exercises every day?"

"Yah,"

"For how long?"

"Mm about 30 minutes usually."

Too inexact to help Visen spot any anomalies that might indicate drowning. She tried to be sensitive to dismissal and peaked back into Moby Dick.

"Do you want to go swimming too sometimes?"

Oh. Nadia really was just that laconic.

"No that's alright,"

"Okay. Just let me know if you do." She went back to patting goo all over her face.

Visen just knew, even if she did keep reading, she'd never finish the sentence she'd already read five times over. "Is that moisturizer?" she hazarded a guess; she'd actually studied to be a biochemist, after a failed attempt at linguistics.

"Yeah; it's retinol with pure Vitamin C extracts to put on after the acai; helps absorb better."

"Cool. So. You enjoy doing make up treatments?"

"No not really."

Okay. So…?

"You just get used to it, like a job, you know? I don't mind it so much; it just gets a bit boring sometimes, y'know? Like I'm so grateful I don't have to work"— *Oh God! Why did she have to say that to a woman who had to work for a living?*— "but sometimes it does get a little boring, y'know, sitting around here all day, doing nothing." *How was she making this worse with every sentence she said?* "I just wish Evelle'd take me on vacation sometimes, y'know." She tried to be relatable. "Like we go to dinner parties and stuff, but I really want to go to Paris, or like, Vienna,"—she sounded Visen out inconspicuously, to see if either city were plebian enough they could find a mutual interest in it. "— y'know something romantic, just us two."

"Ahhh…"

It was suddenly blatantly obvious Visen'd never stepped foot outside Swiverlian Federal territory.

"So. Do you get good vacation hours?"

"Not really," Visen was hoping OPSAI paid good overtime bonuses, though. "Have you ever thought of maybe starting a charity or something?" Wasn't that usually what rich people did when they got bored?

"Uck." Nadia was doing her nails now. Paisley, this time. Visen wasn't even quite sure how she was doing that. Must've been pre-printed—? "Evelle's already got like 18 charities. He's on the phone about them all the time with the Swiverlian government too it's like oh my gawd no just give it a rest; no one wants another school zoning system! They already have a school zoning system! They're all money laundering too, I swear, like, they're not actually, but they don't really ask people what they want, y'know? It's just like 'oh you're poor here have some soccer balls, that'll fix everything.' But I dunno how to actually fix that sort of thing myself, so usually I just keep quiet. I do think charities are overrated though."

"Oh."

Did that sound elitist? "You want some more fruit?"

Chapter 15

The Mertrians came that afternoon, to search Ivle's study for copies of the nuclear fission blueprints he kept swearing originated in no way from himself. Of course, Badmonkof forbade they tip anyone off in advance that they were coming; might give subordinates time to destroy important evidence. They waited until 5, when it was starting to get dark.

Visen saw them just the same, in the CCTV footage on Channel 2. They'd been airlifted over Ivle's gated security to be planted directly in front of a window leading into his office. And she could tell instantly they were Mertrian, because their lookout doubled back to scout out their surroundings only after they'd already started carving a circle out of the glass in Ivle's windowpane. Typical Mertrian. —That was actually protocol.

And of course, they hadn't noticed the private surveillance camera mounted just the other side of the window they were breaking into. They'd also chosen to break into the wrong office…. This was Ivle's casual office, not the one he'd locked Visen out of.

By this time, Nadia had convinced Visen to let her dye her hair, because there was nothing else to do—just the tips, as she was doing the same thing for herself. Nadia considered herself an artist in this field. She didn't want Visen to feel left out.

"You can always cut them off if you don't like the contrast; this is just practice to see if you like it." She went about mixing chemicals and wrapping tinfoil round the sides of Visen's ears while the latter hunched, watching Channel 2 dutifully. She'd just realized if she pressed 'pause' on the TV's remote, she could keep the ever-shifting CCTV footage primed on a single camera of her choice, and she was fiddling round to all the different cameras when she first saw their new interlopers.

—She leaned forward to make sure the Mertrians weren't a trick of the light. Nope. There they were, using standard army glasscutters. So they weren't hiding the fact they were from Mertria….

Should she tell Nadia? She'd promised Ivle not to make her worry.

"You know what," Visen flipped the television back to surveying an innocently un-thief-besieged backdoor. "I think I saw something a bit funny on one of those feeds; I think I'll call Wheeler—"

"Ok but remember we gotta wash your hair out in ten minutes otherwise the chemicals'll burn it—they get kind of sulfur-y,"

Sorry, what was Nadia using to dye their hair again?

Visen turned for the nearest phone—this one, accessible to Nadia, served only as an intercom between security guards.

"Oh— are you having problems seeing through the surveillance cameras?" Nadia thought up a way to continue the conversation as Visen dialed, having noted the footage of the backdoor was looking a bit grainy. "They get kinda dark don't they—?"

"Oh yeah no no just, wanted to check something real fast—"

"Look; so like, for the last interior—the room you were just in, before you switched over?" –(*oh no*)—, "if you want to see brighter you just say 'open lights,' and then the room number: 'open lights 15,'" Nadia spoke into the butt of her TV's remote.

Light flooded into Ivle's casual office. The Mertrians slunk away before the CCTV automatically switched over to viewing the room Nadia'd just remotely commanded. Nadia didn't see them.

They stayed round the corner of a jutting curve in the mansion's east wing, then crept back when enough time had passed for them to assume the lights were only controlled by automatic motion sensors.

"Oh—yeah, that's a lot brighter; thank you; that's nice,"

Wheeler'd just narrated what the intruders were doing from his un-Nadia-hampered CCTV readout.

He'd sensed almost immediately Visen must've been told not to let Nadia know what was happening, the minute he heard Ivle's wife babbling in the background while Visen's phrases became over-generalized.

"Here, I'll come and—"

"Thanks,"

"Look, though," he huffed a bit, speed walking over to the mansion now, cellphone to one ear, "I think you better be the one who goes to see what they want." He knew when he was outclassed; those guys had Berettas. He jogged into the room. "I can stay with—" He pulled up short to point at his own hair, as a way to question what the hell Visen had just done with hers.

"Oh! Highlights. Ok, Nadia? I'll be right back—"

"Is something wrong?" Nadia froze from where she'd been prepping Visen's next aluminum strip.

"No no, just standard protocol; I'll be right back,"

"But the chemicals,"

"Right back,"

"Chemicals?" Wheeler had somehow never made the connection hair dyes involved industrial grade parabens.

"Just two seconds; maybe re-hydrogenate some of the lighter blond for me? I liked that one," Nadia had seven different shades of blond she'd been working with.

"Okay; are you sure?"

"Yeah,"

"I don't think it really goes with your complexion!"

But Visen had already slipped out, locking together a gun as subtly as possible, to avoid Nadia overhearing.

Walker stayed put, watching, mesmerized by the process, as Nadia mixed up a new batch of dyes she'd broken out to complement Visen's choice of blond, against her better judgment.

"You want some?" she indicated the tips of Wheeler's crew cut.

"Oh no—that's—did you say chemicals? I thought that was like bleach not—"

~*~

An unbelievably swift few seconds later, Visen slipped out of a darkened doorway, just behind the Mertrian Special Ops team.

"Can I help you with something?"

From where Ivle sat, overseeing the operation next to Badmonkof via a personnel camera strapped to the third Mertrian on the left, he could see the Mertrians closest Visen jump out of their skin.

Damn she was efficient. She'd levelled her gun just far enough back to cover all five of them, primed to shoot them all in a second. Semi-automatic.

"Let me talk to her—Visen!"

One of the Mertrians handed over his earpiece for her.

"Hello?" she kept her gun leveled straight at them.

"Bravo 2 this is Eagle; we need to enter my study,"

Badmonkof gave Ivle a look. He'd just promised not to pre-alert—

"She has no time to destroy anything! Look—! Visen, give the—earpiece back." The special ops member who'd let her borrow his earpiece stuck it back in his ear again. "Ok, Seagull 2; turn to your left a bit," he pivoted so his body cam showed the study was in fact still devoid of furiously ransacking evidence destroyers.

"Alright." Badmonkof fidgeted.

"Bravo 2 let them in; the correct office. Code 867593," that code changed every night.

"Sir? Permission to verify identity?"

They went through a strictly confidential rigamarole of predetermined countersigns.

Ok, the disembodied voice really was Ivle.

At least, Visen could think up no other objections by which to stall the soldiers' entry.

"You want me to let them in your secured office?"

"Yes,"

"Alright. Come on," she trained them at gunpoint, leading them round to the front door, then in through the atrium—

"No—" Badmonkof poked Ivle's attention away from the third Mertrian's body-cam. "We want—"

"No, they got the wrong office; they landed in front of my spare study; my secret files are actually across the hall."

He hadn't wanted to admit that, but he didn't want Visen asking overly-honest questions, like 'why don't we let them in the one office actually important enough to require a keypad?' Ivle couldn't be sure how much of the Mertrians' mission Visen would eventually intuit, but as head of OPSAI, he was, after all, at least nominally meant to look like he and Badmonkof were on the same side; he didn't need subordinates second-guessing his legitimacy. Not now. "Visen?"

"Yes sir."

They were at the secured office's entryway.

She plugged in the code Ivle'd proffered.

"Why is she wearing tinfoil?" Badmonkof began to worry he'd sensed a trap, perhaps some way to ground

Visen while electrical charge swept away the rest of his team.

"Eh—Vi—Bravo 2 can you explain what you're wearing on your head?"

Not the dye—

"Yeah, I thought my name was never to be given out—"

"I said Bravo 2,"

"You said my name earlier."

"I won't—he won't tell anyone; you won't tell anyone?" Ivle glanced ominously at the president.

"Oh, no. No, no." Badmonkof didn't even remember Ivle'd used a proper name earlier.

Visen hadn't known there was another person in the room with Ivle, listening in to their conversation. She'd just worried the earpiece could be bugged.

"So, what's in your hair?"

"Your wife is dying my hair, sir, to see if I prefer blond highlights."

"Awesome." It was so satisfying knowing Nadia was slowly driving someone else insane too.

Visen maneuvered the intruders through the door that swung open upon successfully entering its passcode, letting them lead the way into the library-like confines of Ivle's secured study.

The room itself was about the length of a modest great hall, with antique books—none of them too antique, to make sure they wouldn't smell—dotting a series of bookshelves stretching down the room's length on both sides, relieved only by small enclaves jutting out to the left to host bay windows and statuettes in a mash-up of ornate and art deco, with cabinets set in the lower half of each bookshelf for housing nonexistent tableware from days when such rooms had actually been used to host dinner parties. Those were the cabinets among which Nadia'd carved out her secret watching niche.

Ivle never touched the bookshelves. Swiverlia, unlike Mertria and Livonia, was fully immersed in the twenty-first century, and more than capable of digitizing all their records for further encryption. There were, of course, always procedures for which official documents had to have hard copies. But one false cabinet amongst the others would never be noticed.

One Mertrian was tasked with copying over all the data on Ivle's home computer, while the rest searched for secondary laptops and, rare as they were, those illusive hard copies of important state secrets.

Visen supposed she could always shoot to kill if one of the intruders came up with anything a little too obviously satisfactory. For now, the fact they couldn't seem to find anything incriminating allowed her the leisure to assume Ivle had in fact given the command to search his rooms, and not just someone pretending to be Ivle, who happened to know her code name, their code identifications, and this night's security code for the study.

Was she being a bit paranoid? She just wanted to do her job well.

"What exactly are you looking for?" she tried to mill casually with a machine gun in her hands.

"Just a review of my paperwork," Ivle was the one to answer that, through the little earbud they'd laid out like a speaker phone. For the next forty minutes he gave Visen several coded combinations to unlock various filing cabinets for the Mertrian team to flip through.

They seemed to be experts at skimming enormous piles of paperwork quickly while tabulating exactly what all those piles contained.

The phone rang.

"Intrahome number sir."

"See what it is,"

"Visen? Hey! We need to take the dye out of your hair or the ends'll split!"

"Ok, I'll be there in a second, alright?"

"Also, the new dye mix is starting to dry."

"Ok."

Ugh—*why* did Visen have to make eye contact at that exact moment with the most judgmental looking searcher? *Like he knew.* Like he could just sense they were talking about the hair-dye. She tried to assume the blank surety of a face perfectly convinced no one could hear Nadia through the landline, to keep up the feeling she fit her performance of the perfectly lethal professional.

"Is everything okay?" Nadia caught her pause.

"Yes, everything's fine; I've just got a few visitors from Ivle—"

Would he be mad she told Nadia that?

"Ooh is it anyone I know?"

"I don't think so, they're—"

"From Badmonkof tell her they're from Badmonkof—" the little earpiece went ballistic, where they'd placed it on a desktop.

"They're from Badmonkof,"

"Ooh; tell him I say hi!"

"Ok. I will. I'm gonna hang up now,"

"Ok I'm gonna try putting the new dyes in the microwave,"

"Ok. I'll be right back." Just a few more stacks, now, probably. "I think. Ok, see you soon."

Visen hung up, gun leveled and pivoting towards anyone who glanced up. Suppose their true motivation was kidnapping Nadia? But they went back to skimming paperwork.

"Oh, and there'll be a few more files in my desk; Bravo 2: codes." Ivle read out the codes for each individually locked drawer. It took about thirty more minutes, before he finally gave the all-clear to usher the Mertrians out again.

Visen was almost sad to see them go.

Chapter 16

The minute the last Mertrian silhouette scrambled up the swinging rope ladder to a retrieval helicopter, the intra-house phone rang again.

It was Wheeler.

"Hey; how do you think we should break it to Nadia, about the break in? Like I know it can be a bit traumatizing for civilians when somebody rifles through their house," he was trying to sound ex-military, scrunching himself into a far corner of the room in hopes Nadia wouldn't hear while she went to wash out one of the ruined dye's receptacles.

"I mean, I already told her I saw something suspicious,"

"Yeah but she's gonna find out they were intruders; I tried to get a window patcher out for the hole they made but the nearest company isn't free till next Wednesday—"

Honestly, dodging Nadia so he could keep an eye on her while at the same time she didn't see the text messages he'd been sending incognito to some window patcher's automated customer service had been almost as hard as babysitting a team of expert data compilers equipped with Berettas.

"I think they might be the only company...." Window Patcher wasn't exactly a well-sought-after job.

"You think she'll get scared if she knows they— were trying to force—?"

"I mean I know I would I'm just assuming,"

"Aah, well, I guess I can explain it to her a bit more thoroughly? They weren't after her...." Who was to say Nadia'd even notice the broken window?

She certainly didn't notice how horrifically Visen's dyed ends had turned out, frizzled into nonexistence— but that may simply have been just trying to be polite.

~*~

"Hey, so," Wheeler joined them for lunch the next day. "I just wanted to check in and make sure you're feeling okay about last night,"

They explained the break in, how normal it was to be a bit frightened by parachuters with grappling hooks…. They showed her the window; they even got permission to re-enter the locked study and show her how the Mertrians attempted restacking everything so it wouldn't look too ransacked.

"So, are you concerned? Is this okay? You feel safe right? You know we're here for you?"

"Oh! Oh my God! Wait, is this all they did? —I thought you guys were like they'd killed somebody or something! No, this kinda stuff happens all the time; it's just Swiverlian politics." Were they not used to this in Mertria? Was that what it meant to be a political backwater? "Do you know what they were looking for?" Nadia leafed through the nearest stack of discarded day to day invoicing, half hoping to find a hard copy of Ivle's faux nuclear reactor plans.

"Um, they were just searching to make sure he didn't have any stolen documents—" or. Something prickled at the back of Visen's mind. They had mentioned something about an original copy—that couldn't possibly corroborate what Nadia'd been saying over dinner that first night, could it? The 'mother' copy? "It was just routine; they didn't find anything worth worrying about—"

"Ooh yeah, no they wouldn't; he puts all that kinda stuff behind his desk— like in the crevice," she mimicked stuffing something.

"Be—what?"

Visen'd seen 'behind' Ivle's desk. She was looking at 'behind' Ivle's desk right now. It was literally a block of black obsidian that rose 7 feet high up the study's right-hand wall.

"—Yeah, like stuff he doesn't want anyone else to find?"

Did Nadia mean the side of Ivle's desk facing his study's entryway? He put his stuff in the side with all the drawers? Visen and Wheeler edged the desk away from the wall an inch, just to make sure. Nothing there. Just an immovable black rock and then the sheer metal backside of the desk itself, devoid of even a rivet to suggest anything other than solid singularity.

Wheeler felt up the inside of the desk's backing, just in case; if he was guarding something infinitely sensitive, he wanted to know. But—nothing taped, no protuberances, no unaccounted-for changes in dimension…. Nadia'd gone on to look through other paperwork, assuming Wheeler's snooping was routine.

"Do you suppose 'secreting office paperwork' could count as grounds for divorce?"

"Uh…Probably not," Visen straightened politely, "if it didn't have anything to do with you personally."

"Yeah, but, like, we're married."

Oh. …kay.

"I mean… you could try it?"

Visen really wasn't well-versed in divorce protocol.

Nadia, on the other hand, had been researching reasonable grounds for divorce ever since she married Ivle, to make sure she didn't fall into any.

That's why she didn't tell them about where the button to reveal the desk's secret compartment was located. Otherwise, Ivle could get her for 'compromising company secrets,' which negated claims to permanent alimony.

"Mm." Nadia made a mental note to ask Jacobsan if accusing Ivle of 'secreting paperwork' could net her more alimony. Maybe emotional damages…. She'd use the spare cellphone Ivle and Visen didn't know about.

Chapter 17

"You know—?" It was now the seventh day, and Ivle showed no signs of intending to keep his promise of returning by the tenth. "We should do something like dying our hair again, that was fun."

Visen'd taken up a sort of sleepy routine; vigilance in no way fully undermined, of course. She still started at every out-of-place noise. But it was more for the sake of keeping herself awake now, than anything else.

"Ok," she roused, "what do you want to do?" She'd already finished Moby Dick. She'd begun to begrudge Nadia her limitless fascination with Cube Bashers.

"I've always wanted to have a girl's weekend! Just us, you know," No drama in the form of a whining husband being dragged along swearing he hated papaya juice.

"Ok," Visen managed to sound encouraging. This entire week had proved much harder than assassinating Colby, as far as the emotional toll it had taken. It really wasn't that bad a way to go—bullet through the head. Visen could only hope that'd be her someday, if she was lucky. If she wasn't, no one would come to put her down and they'd keep questioning her, till her resolve was gone and she counted the seconds—a little bit like… right now.

"What about facial masks? Like really good ones; I've been meaning to try this minted green juniper—"

All the lights went off.

All at once.

Oh thank God!

But also fuck.

Were the Mertrians back?

"Oh God dammit!" Nadia slammed down a powder brush she'd been playing with. Visen jumped about ten feet in the air (she'd been straining her ears for any sounds of forced entry).

TV was down, of course, though power loss automatically initiated an elaborately redundant security system throughout the entire house, which Wheeler'd explained involved having to reboot generators to power in-wall mounts at which one was obliged to provide facial recognition to open any door that'd been closed at the time of the outage.

"I'll kill 'em!" Nadia made a beeline for the stairwell— "Those rotten stupid little fucking bastards—"

"Nadia! No! We don't even know what it—!"

"Oh it happens every damn Thursday night soon as they know Wheeler's off for his break—those little bastards; I'm gonna give em a piece of my mind!"

"No-o-o—Nadia—!"

Wheeler wasn't even supposed to be taking a break—

"We can't just have black outs every Thursday! This isn't Finland!"

"It may not just be the electricity!"

"Well that's why you're here anyway, so it's fine."

Surprising how stiletto-kitty-heels actually slowed Nadia down far less than hastily donning full tactical gear— "Nadiaaa! Don't open the—" too late.

Nadia wrenched open the—practically crenelated— French front doors and stalked out into the night down her driveway—"Nadia!"— Visen slinking after her, running recon while slipping along the open swath of gravel. They were so completely exposed.

Why not check the fuse box?! Maybe it was just a fuse—!

"You!" Nadia shined a flashlight on a man who'd just frozen while sticking a pair of wire-cutting sheers through the bars of a side-fence, attempting to clip at the remaining switches of a box he'd jimmied open with the same tool. "You get away from my breaker boxes!" He cautiously moved the clippers forward anyway— "You get away! From my husband's electricity!" Nadia marched right up to him until they were only a few feet apart: "Don't! You fucking touch that! You get away! You get off my—"

"Look lady I got a seven-inch knife!"

"Yeah and I'm from Brooklyn!"

"Alright," Visen cocked her assault rifle. "Step away from the fence and put your hands up where I can see them." The sheers dropped. "We have a 470," Visen murmured into an intercom on the collar she'd hitched up to one side. 470 meant breach of technological defenses. "Come in main load," (main load was the code name for the little metallic pen at the gate to their driveway).

No one 'came in'. God, what was the use of memorizing specific codes if Ivle's home security was a goddamn nightmare of unprofessionalism?

"I think they might be watching the Super Bowl," Nadia's face warped into a cringy, apologetic 'oops-shoulda-told you that' look.

"You said they've got substitutes," They couldn't *all* be off—

"Ehhh not on Thursdays; Thursdays we just kinda have an arrangement together,"

Nadia gave everyone Thursdays off because it helped her smuggle in whoever she was interested in having sex with that week.

"Ok." Visen returned her attention to the man on the opposite side of her gun. "I don't want you to move. If you move, I shoot," Nadia stayed frozen too, just in case. "Nadia, I need you to go alert Sergeant Wheeler we've had an attempted breaking and entry." At least Wheeler would still be on the premises, right? They housed on-site. He wouldn't go off somewhere random to watch the Superbowl, would he?

"I don't know which one is Sergeant Wheeler?"

"He's the one who's supposed to be in the bullpen tonight," that was what they called the little metallic pen codenamed 'mainload' when they weren't trying to be secretive over coded radio chatter.

"O-oh," Nadia hadn't recognized the epithet 'Sergeant,' "Okay…"

"On second thought…" what if this was a ruse? "Actually, no; stay here; I shouldn't let you out of my sight."

Now Visen had a problem. To retrieve their electricity snapper she would at some point have to hop the fence that appeared to be the only thing keeping him outside the house's actual grounds. Where he'd tripped the breaker, that fence was nothing but iron rods, but that soon gave way to a smooth, stucco finishing closer the driveway, which would actually have been handy for scrambling over if she didn't also need to keep constant visuals on Nadia. Maybe she could threaten him from the Nadia-side of the iron rods with her gun aiming through the fence and force him to walk down along the stucco wall towards the gate—

"Is there a way to open those gates from here?"

"No, it doesn't open; it's not a gate it's just a fence,"

"No, I mean the gate at the front of the drive,"

"Oh. I mean, honestly this happens every Thursday night; he's been trying it for quite a while now." Maybe they could just let him go.

"Trying to do what?"

"I dunno; get in, I guess,"

Hm. Thursday was when Ivle had his scheduled mandatory OPSAI conference with Swiverlian cabinet members, a fact Visen only knew from the first-hand experience of having had to appear at quite a few of these meetings herself to give reports. That meant whoever was trying to break in was part of Swiverlian government, or at least privy to the meeting schedule Swiverlian government forced on OPSAI.

Why had no one mentioned this problem before?

Visen had a sudden, horrid realization Nadia must not have deemed it important enough to tell her husband. "Sergeant Wheeler we have a 470," she switched attention to her hand held, "come in. Come in Sergeant Wheeler!" He was supposed to have an emergency radio, always—!

"I think he's watching the Superbowl."

"Well, yeah but—"

Come to think of it, Nadia wanted to be watching the Superbowl too. She'd forgotten that was on tonight. Maybe that's what they should do for their girl's weekend, soon as they'd recalibrated all the damn door locks…. "I think we should just let him go." the perpetrator had already taken several inconspicuous steps back, as though to suggest he agreed with this plan.

"You stay where you are!" Inconspicuous backing stopped. "Tell me your name!"

"Fuck you!"

That was not a name.

"Tell me who you work for!"

The perpetrator just shrugged sarcastically. Okay. Visen wasn't great at this more extraverted side of small-arms deployment.

"If you want," Nadia was analyzing, "you can walk on the wall down to where the gate is, and then you can keep an eye on him, and I'll walk down along beside you, and then I can open the gate, and you guys can both come in,"

"Okay," the top of the wall's stucco portion was flat, where it began about three meters to their left. "Ok, take ahold of this; I want you to cover him while I get up top," Visen schooled Nadia in how to aim at their prisoner. "Alright. You got that?"

By the time she'd hopped up on the wall he was gone. "What the—?" Nadia had shifted the butt of the rifle to under her armpit for better access to siting along its barrel. Oi.

"You're not in cahoots with him or anything by any chance—?"

"No, but it is just a breaker switch, we can turn it back on real easy; he never gets to cutting through the plastic part so all he ever really does is flip the switch off—"

"I don't think we should go out there—" What if clipper boy had back up? Visen couldn't take chances without the risk Nadia'd be left without any security at all.

"No it's okay; I know his wife. His name's Desmond. He goes to the same Federal Reserve Balls as Evelle."

Oh.

So this was Swiverlian government, doing the raiding then.

Great. Had this one been sanctioned by Ivle as well? To keep Visen on her toes? Had she just committed a federal offense by aiming a gun at the perpetrator? Guy hadn't produced a warrant.

"Has he ever told you what he plans to do if he does get inside, besides cut the power supply?"

"No, but he's probably after the newest list of insurgents; everybody's always trying to doctor that list, like if one of their cousins got on it or something. That's why they give it to Evelle; he doesn't have any living family." Hm. Might explain a thing or two. Ivle was also rich enough the common man couldn't offer a bribe that'd interest him.

Visen scrambled back down from the wall, feeling stupid. Maybe they could go get Wheeler to help them reset the breaker together: one to guard Nadia, one to fiddle at circuits. Nadia went over just to make sure her hand couldn't reach the breaker through the fence's bars.

"So, Ivle keeps a list of Swiverlian 5th columnists?" This was the first Visen'd heard of any insurgency taking place in Swiverlia. She thought that was only in Mertria, her home country's unique, sort of perpetual faux pas.

"Yeah, any insurgents in any of the autonomous zones; he writes it up every Wednesday." Oh, so that's why Desmond attacked Thursdays, not OPSAI's meeting—

"Ivle writes it?"

"Yeah, he's head of secret police; that's pretty much all he ever does." Nadia'd always assumed all the Bravos were part of the secret service that worked under Ivle.

"Oh." Of course. Swiverlia *would* plant secret police to head up Mertria's only quasi-chance to self-govern their own integration into the Federation, wouldn't they?

Well, no wonder, then. Visen'd thought Ivle seemed a bit paranoid for a purely civilian leader of OPSAI, Peace Task Force.

Must have been all the covert secret service executions he kept authorizing, getting him jumpy.

That would also explain how he'd gained access to all the information he needed to blackmail Visen. And why the Swiverlians at her Bonmount Acour obeyed a simple flick of his hand—

"Were you not supposed to know that?"

"Uh, honestly, I just work freelance for him; I thought he was just a consultant."

"O-oh. Don't tell him I told you then."

"Right. No, lips are sealed."

Chapter 18

Now, was there any way to report Wheeler for abandoning his post to go watch the Superbowl? Even if Nadia authorized….

He finally strolled up about ten minutes later.

They decided, as fitting retribution, it should be Wheeler who had to go out beyond the gate to fix the feeder switch, in its painfully infiltrate-able little secondary fenced in enclosure, just the other side of any truly enforceable security measures.

"Will you—I mean—what if he's still out there?"

"That's your fault! I'll cover you."

He fiddled for an abnormally long amount of time.

Nadia was starting to get visibly cold; the hair all along her arms had arched as she rubbed at them while shifting from side to side.

"He has no idea what he's doing out there does he?"

"I don't know; it's just a generator switch isn't it?"

Visen crunched disappointed gravel over to instruct the Sergeant on how best to flip at a switch-panel. At least it was obvious which switch they were aiming for, the one with small plier indents all round its corners. "Ok." Visen continued to keep an eye on Nadia, aware, every moment, of the quickest path by which to close the distance between the two of them, should kidnappers materialize. But this was no ruse on Wheeler's part. Apparently, he'd lived in a duplex his whole life, and the landlord hadn't trusted tenants with access to the breaker boards. He hadn't noticed only one switch was turned the wrong way. "Yeah you had to call in whenever the power went out," *Really?* What was wrong with people?

"Alright."

At long last, the iron gate clanged shut behind them, locking everyone back inside.

"Well, that was a fun girl's night out wasn't it?"

Awkward silence followed, as Wheeler waited to be fired. Pity Visen didn't have the authority. She could always call Ivle—

"So," Nadia turned to walk back inside, "you guys wanna go watch the Superbowl?"

Nadia always watched it mainly for the commercials.

They'd worry about the in-wall facial recognition later. They could always simply fail to boot up the generators tonight and sleep mercifully unguarded.

"You know she could have been kidnapped," Visen took Wheeler aside, as soon as it was evident they were descending into the little break room for guards Nadia was apparently very familiar with—

"Oh please; she's not gonna get kidnapped; no one wants that kinda shit on their hands; Ivle's wife? Absolute death sentence."

"So—what? You think he's just trying to isolate her?"

"Yeah; 'she's not supposed to talk to strange men,'" he mimicked; he'd gotten that order too.

"Do you count as strange?"

"Honestly yes, but I don't think he thought of that,"

Another guard got Visen a beer. "Patriots are down two to zero,"

"Thank you," this meant absolutely nothing to Visen, but she appreciated feeling as though she were included.

"Whe-ee-ler! Do you have whiskey?"

Oh so now Nadia did know which one was Wheeler….

Maybe she just didn't know to refer to him as Sergeant— that was a Mertrian security title…. "We should play a drinking game!"

Ah. So, this was what Nadia got up to when her husband wasn't around.

Flirting with the entire security team en masse. She'd already cuddled up next to the best looking of Wheeler's subordinates.

"Ai! Yeah yeah—" Wheeler went off searching for hard liquor, as Nadia explained she didn't like beer.

Oh no; why did they have to invite Visen to join in? This was so uncomfortable. She felt foolishly rigid as she sat there on the side couch all night, drinking beer, knowing alcohol could never bypass the silence that had long since fallen over her capacity to reciprocate small talk.

"That's because you need whiskeyy—" Nadia inserted herself as soon as Visen tried to apologize for her own personality, replacing the beer with Jack Daniels. "Soo never have I ever during commercial breaks—"

"It's a kid's game—"

"Yeah I'm bored! Sexy here goes first."

The security guard beside her shuffled his torso up into good posture, looking exaggeratedly self-important to play off the compliment.

"I thought I was sexiest!"

"I didn't say sexiest I said sexy!"

"I'm sexiest!"

Visen hadn't even noticed they had a fifty-year-old groundskeeper in there with them, who kept winking at Nadia.

"Yeah, ok, no, we can all agree Josan and his wife are the sexiest couple in the world," everyone cheered.

Okay. So actually, this was just how Nadia acted when she felt comfortable around people. Made sense, Visen supposed. Her entire life was a carefully balanced sex act for her husband; flirting was apparently just how she made friends.

"Yeah no, I swear Ivle's just paranoid," drunk Wheeler settled back into the conversation he'd been having with Visen earlier. "Like, have you seen the weird defense system for when the lights go out?"

"I dunno, if people are breaking in so often—"

"No no, but it's like a personality thing with him,"

Seemed Wheeler wanted to gossip about Ivle almost as much as Nadia did. Lucky, that. Visen could think up appropriate responses, when conversation remained work related. "What do you mean personality?"

"Like, he's so scared there's gonna be some sort of leak he took Nadia's texting abilities away," very irritating that; Wheeler and Nadia always texted. (She could be friends without knowing names!) "And why? Probably because of that Colby guy,"

"They told you about that?"

"Yeah well they had to bring the body back out to bury him," no use forensics finding a slug from the rifle Ivle exclusively equipped OPSAI teams with. "But honestly? That whole thing was just dumb luck. That was just that Smutt guy making a lucky guess Colby'd have something on Ivle because he was pissed, because they wouldn't let him into their secret little conference! But Ivle thinks it's this whole like, grand damn conspiracy thing; I know he does; one Bravo flips and he's like 'oh my God everyone's after me!' But like, no I was there, I saw it; it was spur of the moment; it wasn't thought out; it was literally just one guy being like 'you know what? I think this would work.' But no one ever asks me anything,"

"Aw yeah it's always a lot stupider than people assume, isn't it?"

"Yeah! Exactly!"

See? This was fun. Visen was having a conversation, just relaxing with the guys. (Nadia counted as one of 'the guys' because by 'the guys' Visen's mentality meant anyone not psychopathically driven enough to become the first female Mertrian SEAL to win the Bonmount Acour.)

~*~

"Ah, yeah, we're all good friends," Nadia explained at one in the morning, as she and Visen finally wound their way back up to the main house, four whiskeys deep. "I'm so glad you were there to rescue me with that gun though; You're such a pro!" She walloped her entire body sideways in an enthusiastically light tap against Visen's left shoulder to hug her.

"Like, I can't believe the look on Desmond's face when I came out with you toting that rifle; that was so perfect! Usually I just have to call the police," (using her secret phone Ivle didn't know about).

"I'm glad I could help!"

"Oh, my gawd you were so great; I want that every time now! And you look so good in those fatigues too, like tough is so sexy, you know?" Yup, flirting was how she made friends.

"Oh, thank you," It was the first time anyone'd ever considered Visen capable of being a sexual creature in her own right, as though it were something voluntary and external to herself, that she could put on for her own benefit, and take off as she wanted. She didn't wear make-up. And stress from on the job encouraged countless blemishes, that were slowly being added to by wrinkles. "—I've actually been a little self-conscious about my acne recently," (was this what normal people talked about together after four whiskeys?)

"Awh no! We'll fix that,"

"Ok,"

"I have just the mask!"

"Cool. So, you never told your husband about the whole Desmond thing?"

"No, I only tell him stuff if I need his help; also, I don't want to get Desmond in trouble, because he's already bankrupted twice and Nori's thinking of leaving him. Like it would be awkward for her if he was convicted, y'know?"

"Fair enough."

What else was Nadia hiding, though?

Well, a way to by-pass the entire facial-recognition system for one thing; apparently after you showed your face to two of the cameras there was an 'ALT-ALL' button you could press. Seemed very easily riggable by clever kidnappers. All you had to do was present her face—why was this—?

"Oh I swear this is just to collect data sampling for how faces age, so he can create a program to track people,"

"Oh." That was a conspiracy theory Visen could almost believe, though if it were true, Nadia's anti-wrinkle serums must be playing havoc with the algorithms....

"Hey, you know, I like you; this has been really fun; like I don't usually get to have girl friends," she kissed Visen on the cheek. "You'll leave the surveillance panel open, won't you?" They'd reached their rooms.

"Always do."

"Thank you! Wait—" she pulled Visen to her and kissed her fully on the lips, dead on. "Thank you." She hugged her, one tight squeeze. "I do really like you, you know,"

"I like you too," Visen was surprised to find the words came easily; they weren't solely politeness.

"So, would you ever be interested in—y'know,"

Nadia's hand had stayed on Visen's chest; now she shimmied her curves up against Visen like a joke, but it was amazing how soft they were, as though the two were meant to meld together.

"Aheh—" Visen's curve to one side came as a 'ho, no I don't think so—' but she caught herself. "I mean— um, not opposed," She didn't want to let Nadia down; she'd regret it.

Nadia kissed her again, slower this time, with all the luscious practice of over-pumped up lips.

The sensation—so sudden— was halfway to orgasm but entirely in the region of the mind, a mental joy, as though Visen's heart and thoughts had jumped as one in excitement at unexpected arousal.

"You like that? Maybe we should try doing it more often, yeah?"

"Okay," Visen managed to smile, her whole consciousness focused on the thrill that Nadia's hand was trailing down her fatigues towards their belt.

Did that merit a bullet through the brain? Kissing Ivle's wife? Probably….

"We've got three more days you know,"

"Yeah," Visen hadn't realized she'd gripped Nadia's waist to pull her closer, as Nadia reached round to play at the buttons on the back of her pockets.

"Well—" Nadia didn't want to come on too strong too quickly, "goodnight!" she grinned, nodded, then slipped behind the door to her bedroom, absolutely thrilled.

"Goodnight!"

Chapter 19

Visen woke the next morning to 17 sausages.

"Wheeler suggested you might like them!"

Yes! This was actually exactly the breakfast Visen'd wanted for ages. She had a feeling she was being bribed for keeping silent about the whole 'not-showing-up-for-an-intruder' thing.

Nadia was having fruit again. "Do you want some?"

"No thanks," (Visen wondered vaguely if it was the same crystal bowl that kept following them around or if there were multiple versions in different rooms....)

"It's supposed to be good for your complexion y'know,"

"Ah, un-huh?" *Continues shoveling sausages.*

"Here, I'll tell you what! We should do a facial," the happy shoveling of sausages stopped.

"Like a—?"

"Like for your face; It'll help get rid of lines too," Nadia pointed to the smile lines that were beginning very faintly to appear on her own cheeks.

"Oh ok."

Visen no longer felt quite as attracted to Nadia.

More importantly, Nadia didn't seem to remember they had kissed each other the night before.

Except for when she winked, when she brought out all her face masks.

"So, we have charcoal, avocado..."

There was something funny about Nadia, so lithe, like she couldn't possibly have thought Visen took her seriously enough to be affected by one kiss. For another thing, she mixed all her own cosmetics. That was unexpectedly impressive.

"You know, if I did do a charity, like you were saying—" they didn't have a whole lot of mutual conversations to fall back on— "maybe that's what I'd do, help ladies get rid of lines and wrinkles." Nadia began lathering green goo over Visen's poker face.

"Oh; uh-huh," this felt like congealed ice; there was probably mint in it. Why was Visen letting her do this? Drunk kisses meant nothing; Nadia was just a flirt. *Put it out of your mind*.

"Yeah no but it helps, I mean, look at me; you think I'd be here if I had wrinkles all over my face?"

"Oh—I'm sure your husband cares for you more than y'know, a few wrinkles,"

"Ah don't play dumb; it's unbecoming. My mom used to always say that: don't play dumb. She always told me if I didn't know something, it was better just not to talk about it," Nadia went off to mix some more anti-wrinkle moisturizer. She honestly didn't mean it as an injunction for Visen to shut up. She never even noticed that's the way it might have been construed. "Ok, there. Now you leave that on for fifteen minutes and the feverfew'll decrease cytokine release, which'll make your skin less puffy, and it'll help prevent damage to your DNA from the sun. This is unparthenolided too so it's much easier on your skin," she pushed Visen to lean back into her chair while putting up ointments.

"I think I should probably keep sitting up,"

"No, it sets better if you don't fight gravity,"

"I'm technically on duty until four," she and Wheeler had swapped night and day duties; he'd wanted to sleep in after the Super Bowl.

"Oh no, don't worry, no one ever comes in, except Desmond, and he can't get through the fence bars; they're Titanium; also electrified; like, not a whole lot but if you try to clip 'em, it'll melt your tools, or something—I'm not quite sure,"

Sounded intense. Visen leaned back slowly until she was lying flat out on her spare pool-side recliner, staring up at the Solarium ceiling. She still felt perched and uncomfortable; girls' weekends were so entirely foreign to her. She was pretty sure they were foreign to anyone who actually—

"Did you hear that?" she snapped back up, in a nervously quickened lean forward.

"Yeah the TV short-circuited," Nadia was blinking up at the flatscreen she kept above the pool. She kept TVs on in all the rooms; it was one of her little habits Visen secretly found absolutely atrocious. But this TV, at least, Visen had managed to convince her to leave on the peacefully unobtrusive quiet of the silent surveillance feed. Nadia got up and found a remote to flip through its channels. All the other channels were working just fine.

Oh my God. How many people were going to try to break into this house?

"Shit." Now they were alone in a 50-room mansion with no central nervous system to see how precisely alone they were—once again. And the tingling mintiness smeared over Visen's face kept distracting her from thinking clearly.

She hadn't realized how much she'd miss Channel 2 till it was gone!

Her hand went to the omnipresent Glock she kept by her side even in sleep. Listening intensified…. Nothing but a far-off AC.

"Is that Desmond?"

"No, he's never been able to do that before."

"Has this happened before?"

"I dunno; I don't usually keep the security channel on."

Great.

Visen could just bet none of the late-sleeping security guards had ever noticed this anomaly before either.

Some sort of timed— maintenance?

But Wheeler hadn't forewarned her.

And no one was calling it in now; no one else must've noticed. Could the CCTVs in the guards' house not have been affected?

A kidnapper *would* cut access to CCTV monitors only inside the mansion, wouldn't they? —To keep a security team stationed routinely at an external gatehouse from noticing anything had gone wrong; feed 'em repeated images that anyone in-house would know instantly didn't match the reality of who was in what room.

Or could whoever did this simply know Wheeler and his team were still asleep?

Still, cutting access to only one channel… something about the exactness of that premeditated duplicity gave Visen the sinking feeling whoever was trying to break in now might not be there at Ivle's bequest.

Maybe she and Wheeler'd been a bit too hasty to discount Ivle's fears. Course, given the track record so far, maybe she should call Ivle to confirm it really wasn't Mertrians again—though if there was danger, she didn't have time to take a break from remaining fully alert.

"Do you think it's Desmond? I really don't think it's Desmond; he's never been able to do anything like this before,"

"No, I don't think it's Desmond. Your husband doesn't know about Desmond, but he still hired me."

"Who was he worried about?"

"I dunno." Insurgents? This far south?

"Would they have access to technology specialists?"

"I don't know but we should probably keep as quiet as possible just in case they do,"

Good thing the solarium walls were made entirely of glass—!

Except those connecting the room to the rest of the house—that actually was a lucky break. Maybe; if their visitor was already inside.

Visen slunk to go stand by the Solarium door, Nadia slinking to stand beside her. "Do you think it's related to Desmond?" she whispered really loudly.

"I don't know," Visen mouthed, hoping to lead by example. A crash and a tinkle somewhere very close by led them both back to staring at the door. Visen wished she hadn't chosen the Glock for active day service. Maybe a T578....

She did, however, still have thermal vision goggles with her—

They slopped right into her facial when she tried to put them on.

"O-oh—God Damnit." Must not. Get mad— at the mintiness. Nadia somehow silently procured a towel without moving.

"Thank you,"

"Although, technically, you're not supposed to rub your face with terry cloth, you're just supposed to pat it, like— just— pat,"

Hmm. Visen's was the only face Nadia'd ever seen come out blotchier than it'd been before she put the mask on. She blamed the terry cloth, definitely not her fault.

"Oh—God." Visen stooped minute moodiness to the precision of cleaning out the thermal-vision goggles too. No. More. Avocado. Ok. There; she put them back on.

There was no one in the surrounding three floors for thirty yards. God this place was ginormous. Someone, though, appeared to be sneaking around the fourth floor to the west; Visen could pick up their heat signature very faintly as they dis- and re-appeared between the load-bearing poles in the house's central walls.

"There's someone just about at the other end of the house; diagonal from us; so like, if the house is this square," she made a square with her hands, "we're here, and they're there. Do you know what room that could be?"

"…No."

Well, at least Nadia was honest.

"Ok it may be nothing but I'm gonna try to keep an eye on them,"

"Should we go ask them what they're doing? Maybe it's the cook,"

"No, the cook's off after 10,"

"Oh. That doesn't mean it couldn't be the cook,"

Ok. "Fair point." Nadia must have been used to people discrediting her ideas. She beamed.

It didn't feel safe to focus all attention on that one form though; were there others? Perhaps screened by structural supports. Visen had never fully appreciated open-plan housing before now.

"Maybe it's the TV repair man,"

"Did you have a TV repair man scheduled for today?"

"No, but sometimes they come out to fix the cable unexpectedly."

Could Wheeler have let them in? He did live on site.

"Ok. Do you have anywhere safe where you could lock yourself in momentarily while I scout this out? Remember Ivle feared they'd be after you, so if there is trouble, we need to be sure they can't find you; that's top priority; doesn't matter what else they take."

But Nadia had Ming vases in that part of the house….

"…Do they have goggles like the ones you're wearing?"

If they did, they worked for Ivle, because these were technically a prototype.

"I don't think so."

"Ok. Yeah, I can think of a place to hide,"

"Ok but it can't just be hiding I mean like do you have a safe room or anything—?"

"Yeah I had it installed when I redid my bathroom,"

"Really?" *Oh my God that was awesome!* "Why?"

"I dunno there was room for it,"

"Ok let's go there now,"

Yes, there was definitely something strange about Nadia.

They slipped out of the Solarium, leaving its door open, and moved, one leg over the other, sideways down the hallway in tactical readiness.

Nadia's high heels kept echoing.

"I think maybe it'd be better if you—"

"Oh yeah right," she slipped them off and wiggled pedicured toes to promise echoing footsteps would not happen again. "Sorry I thought if I moved the same way you did it wouldn't make any noise—"

"Wait, you've been—? Oh—you don't—need to—do that with the arms out in front if you're not holding a gun,"

"Oh; arms out in front isn't for balance?"

"I mean, it, can be," oh gawd she didn't want to make her feel stupid. "Ok, where's your bathroom?"

"This way—"

"I think I should go first,"

"Ok. 2nd left."

"Wh—"

"The doorway with the pheasants,"

"Got it,"

"Ok. Now, 3rd right. Yeah down—yeah that's right, down two floors. Third archway on your left. Ok turn right."

"Nadia." This was the room the intruder was in.

He was still in it.

Visen gave Nadia the thermal-imaging cap, so she could take a look.

"Oh. Same guy?" Well, Visen hadn't seen anyone else and he'd been in that room every 30 seconds when she checked back in on him. She'd been worrying they were getting a bit close.

"So maybe it is just the TV guy,"

"I don't think we should go in just in case it's not,"

Visen never thought she'd be explaining something so quietly in all her life.

"Ok do you still want to go to the safe room? That's not my bathroom he's in, that's just the bedroom, my bathroom's off to the left, see? I think you can see the pipes with the thermal thing."

Oh, you could see the pipes.

"Is there a way to get to your bathroom without going through your bedroom?"

"…No,"

"And you can only get into the safe room from the bathroom?"

"Yeah…." Nadia realized the design flaw. "I think we should chance it it's probably just the TV guy,"

"Why's he been in your bedroom for fifteen minutes?" It'd taken them a while to slink over.

"He always does my TV first; I asked him to."

"Ok but what does—" oh. Normal hardware for cable network television might not need to be checked up on all that often, but Visen could imagine Ivle's secret service teams keeping tabs periodically on how well all his surveillance monitors were functioning.

"Ok. I'll go in." Visen was now communicating mainly through hand gestures. "You stay out here and start backing down the hallway," she made another sweeping scan of the surrounding rooms with her thermals, to make sure no one else was lurking. "Make your way out back, towards Wheeler's cabin if anything goes wrong, okay?" Nadia would have a clear shot towards safety that way. And if Wheeler wasn't in, someone else would be. Visen could see at least two sleeping thermal forms fighting off the vestiges of a hangover in there. "Start backing now, and check through these—" she handed over the thermal goggles, "every few seconds to make sure no one's in an adjoining room." She waited until she was satisfied Nadia was far enough away not to be seen. "Alright."

Bang. She kicked the door in at the bolt. It went flying round to crack the wainscoting. "Freeze! Security! Who are you?" A shadowy figure in black parkoured up the nearest of Nadia's four poster beds, through the surveillance panel Visen'd left open— "Dammit!"—but not before Visen could see he was armed. He'd have a clear view of the path to Wheeler's from upstairs.

Quick! She whipped round in time to catch Nadia just about to slink backwards down a stairwell. "Nadia! here; now!" again, predominately hand gestures, supplemented by completely unaspirated vocals.

"Got it!" (thumbs up), "what's up? All good?" She'd slunk back over the blissfully muffling carpet.

"Get in the safe room!" Visen kept her gun pointed at the surveillance panel. Nadia calibrated.

"Got it! Ok!" She ran. Into the bathroom. A certain amount of scraping could be heard, then nothing. Visen backed slowly towards the sound, eyes locked on the surveillance panel's looming maw in the ceiling. She peaked a second behind her at the assorted hairspray and body soaps that lined the bathroom. Nothing looked out of place. Where'd Nadia gone? Oh god. "Nadia?" She didn't dare call out louder than a hiss—

"Do you need the thermal imaging goggles?" A panel at the back of the lowest of seven shelves by the bathtub slid up to reveal Nadia peering up at Visen from behind folded towels.

"Put it down put it back down!' Visen signaled desperately. The panel closed. Now it looked like a normal shelf for towels again. On second thought, Nadia slid the panel open halfway again and inched the thermal-imaging headgear out millimeter by millimeter until it balanced atop the nearest stack of towels. Then she closed the panel again.

Visen inched—inched—cuffed one arm round quick to snag the goggles while still keeping eyes and gun sighted on the panel-hole in the bedroom.

Thermals on, she could tell the perp had disappeared from the floor above. She swiveled round. Now someone was coming down the hall. Smaller, different build. Three men were just behind him, following the same trajectory towards her.

They seemed to be combing every room for inhabitants as they went along. On the floor below, six more figures were doing the same thing.

"There's a whole lot of them out there isn't there?" It sounded like the bathtub was talking to her, slightly muffled.

"You saw them?" Visen came to kneel down by its little claw feet.

"Yeah through the thermal,"

"Ok, don't worry; they're still quite far away."

"Ok but there's like 20 of them and they'll get real suspicious if you go out in a blaze of glory defending a bathroom; you should get in here with me,"

"I think I should go get help,"

"You can text from in here; I brought my phone. You can hide it behind the towels and still get reception,"

How did Nadia know all this? (Spying; lots of spying. On Ivle). *Did this usually happen when Ivle was out of town?*

"Your phone can't text,"

"No, my other phone."

Visen ought to have known….

"Besides, it'll be better to hide because then we can see what they're up to,"

She had a point there. If the hunch Visen shared with Wheeler was right, and Ivle's plan was focused more on keeping Nadia silent than on keeping her safe, these people could be after something entirely unrelated to Visen's worries as a bodyguard. She might be able, at least, to find out where they came from, based on the tactics they used.

Ok; she would spy. But to feel responsible she'd also alert Wheeler to get the damn creepers out of the house as quickly as possible, opportunities to spy be damned. "Ok; I'll come in." There was a light knocking and the panel rose up again. "Is there enough room for two?"

"Oh yeah it's huge,"

At least this could buy some time. Glok in first. Then shoes off. Shoes in. Towels aside. Snake through. Towels back in place. Panel lowered. Thermal vision back on—

"Wait. These walls aren't metal,"

"So?"

"If they do have thermal devices, they'll be able to see us."

"O-oh…. Right."

Of course, if they did have thermal vision devices that worked well enough to see during the day, they were definitely working for Ivle; that'd add a weird twist.

Visen ought to have known by 'safe-room' Nadia wouldn't mean industry-standard requirements.

"Did you soundproof it?"

"I don't—think so, no."

She had painted it blue, though.

Oh shit. They were in a death trap, weren't they? Visen snuck her fingers and phone out a hopefully inconspicuous crack at the bottom of the towel shelf, as Nadia held the panel open, and began texting quickly for back up. She called as well, pushing the buttons without getting her ear close to the phone, and letting it ring till she saw Wheeler'd picked up, to make sure she got his attention. Then she hung up to maintain silence and continued texting instructions.

'Got it; police called; reinforcements on way now'— plus a little thumbs up emoticon.

Really?

Nadia's safe room was just tall and wide enough you could sit or stand comfortably but standing meant Visen's Glock wouldn't be poised perfectly to fire should anyone manage to come through the towel rack's lowest panel. Then again, if they hacked in through the wall, standing up would give Visen more of an advantage in the initial on-slot.

She ended up pressing her back against the little room's side wall in one perpetually enduring squat, Glock poised to aim at the sliding panel, but easily drawn up to shoot through the walls as well.

Then she went back to scanning via the thermals: now to the right; now, behind and in front of them.

17 thermal blobs had converged in what appeared to be a sweep and search.

So Ivle's fears weren't just an excuse to keep Nadia from gossiping away inflammatory secrets—and they weren't paranoid. Visen could only hope the man she'd interrupted in Nadia's room had interpreted her stomping out again to collect Nadia as a stomp out to flee the building. They'd been as quiet as possible sneaking back into Nadia's. Could be rather a good thing the surveillance cameras had been cut, after all. Hopefully, no one would know they were still present.

It took a few head-swivels, thermal goggles still on, but it did eventually dawn on Visen that Nadia appeared to have pressed her entire face flat against the wall to their right. Visen took off the mask, just to be sure. Nope, face still full on flat against the wall.

"Nadia?" She poked. Nadia pivoted invitingly to point at a hole in the wall, about head sized, in the shape of a keyhole.

Oh, so that's where her nose had gone.

At the hole's center, a true keyhole streamed light. Nadia'd taken a little preconfigured chunk out of the wall. She'd made it keyhole shaped and centered its cutting on the actual keyhole of the faux cabinet just beyond, to make her peephole more aesthetically pleasing.

"Wha--?"

"Go on,"

Visen peered through.

It was Ivle's study. The one with no CCTVs, that he kept stringently locked.

"He usually cheats on me in here so I've used this sometimes to catch him," Nadia explained, whispering a thumbs up. Come to think of it, Nadia'd originally installed the hideaway to catch him cheating with none other than Bravo 2— or Bravo 1— whatever Ivle called Visen.

How on earth had Badmonkof's men not found out about this?

From the peephole's vantage point, it appeared to be on a par with the line of cabinets that ran round the base of Ivle's library-esque floor-length bookshelves. Hadn't they searched those? The fake backing's keyhole-shaped chunk must exhibit exquisitely invisible joinery—

One of the five searchers on their floor peeled off from where the intruders had apparently been holding an impromptu council, and began making his way, Glock raised, down the bookcases that lined the opposite wall of Ivle's study.

"How the hell'd he get in? We locked it!"

"Sh—"

There were niches inset between bookcases every three meters, and before each of these the man wouldd methodically tense, then relax to find that the only forms hiding between shelves were replica busts of Cicero and other high thinkers, down through the ages to Galileo. No desperate housewives.

He turned towards the computer.

—"Shiiit." —

But he bypassed it entirely, with a single sweep down to look under the desk. No groping after faux paneling, the way Visen and Wheeler had. Just a quick look.

So, they weren't looking for paperwork this time, that was definite. Visen could hear radios click through the wood paneling. 'Ground floor swept.'

'Copy that search the tennis courts.'

They were local. That accent was common in Jolinta.

Someone was looking under the bed in Nadia's room as well. If it came to it, Visen'd shoot the library guy first—she was standing in between Nadia and the bedroom's searcher—then she'd shoot the bedroom searcher. She squatted, primed.

'West wing's bedrooms both vacant.'

'Copy that.'

Yeah, they were definitely searching for Nadia; they weren't focusing on main data-dumps.

How had they gained access, though? Visen put an eye to the nook's faux keyhole, to watch as the man in the library finished his sweep. He was walking back towards the main stairwell now, face entirely cloaked in the drape of a 1950s French frogman's uniform, tucked into the pitch-black suit that covered everything else, save his gun.

Visen rechecked visuals on all their other thermal buddies. There were thirty of them now. —*Please let some of those be Wheeler's backup crew*. They were! She told Nadia: two men down by the front door had attacked a third. The other searchers hadn't noticed; Wheeler's guys must've incapacitated their target's radio.

Quick, what could Visen tell about the others, based on how they operated, before they were interrupted? The frogman gear was a standard design released into the public domain in 2006; she'd used it herself on recon operations. But it wasn't affiliated with any official military operating today; no military'd authorize using that antiquated a design. That meant these men were most likely operating under the radar; not officially allied. So, this was private politics, not official Swiverlian intrigue.

Wheeler's security team and their back up had started clearing out rooms in earnest now; altercations broke out a floor above and about three rooms down.

Chapter 20

Oh, this was so irritating; Visen wanted to help! Could she sneak out—? An awful risk…. "They've started picking off stragglers," she handed over the thermal-vision for Nadia to see for herself.

"Ooh." this was kinda cool. "I hope they don't hurt anyone too much,"

"Yeah…."

That sweep and search tactic though, that wasn't standard Swiverlian, despite the Jolinta accent. It wasn't standard Mertrian either, at least not how the SEALs had learned it. They weren't using partners, though that may only have been because they weren't expecting resistance.

The one in the office, though, he certainly hadn't been well trained. On the other hand, parkouring up a bed post probably took lots of training. Could it be two separate groups? A coincidence? Just how many entities were interested in trying to kidnap Nadia?

"Oooh…" Nadia pivoted her head to watch as one home invader raced the length of a hall above them, invisible to Visen.

"What's happening?"

"Shh— oh shit this just got— o-ooh! Oh man, this guy's still trying to get away—I think one group's clearing out the other. I mean like successfully, like you were saying, not just trying." By the time Visen redonned the goggles there wasn't much left to see. Someone was running down a back staircase

"Are there any staircases in this house that lead directly to an exit?"

"Hm?"

Thermal handed back over.

"Mmm. Yeah that one leads outside. You're thinking of going and getting him?"

"Maybe; it might help with questioning; we could find out who they are—"

"They already got a guy on the fifth floor,"

"Oh, shit really?" She shouldn't have let Nadia borrow the thermal visioning for so long.

"Yeah it was like three against one,"

"Okay."

"Can we be sure those guys are Wheeler's?"

"No-o. –Good point. Not absolutely; I'll text him," Panel up.

~Bwoop~ (little sendy sound.)

'Clearing Upper Stories Now,'

Oh. So, Wheeler was one of those people who capitalized everything; Visen hadn't noticed that before now.

"It's them," she double checked with thermals to make sure action played out as Wheeler claimed.

"Ok, cool. So, I guess you should stay here a while longer with me, right?"

"I was thinking they might need help,"

"You're not gonna leave me alone though, are you? I'm the one they're after, right?"

Ah. "Yeah, no, you're right—that's a—good point."

But Visen had been wanting to see if she was still in fighting shape…. She'd been so lax the past week.

But of course, didn't want straggling antagonists to cause last minute chaos by catching Nadia while on the run. "Yeah, I should stay, ok." Visen relinquished cellular reception and crowded back into the little hidden room, back into her squat, gun poised.

"Let me know if anyone comes back into the study okay?"

"Got it." Nadia took up sentry duty through the keyhole, squatting in a semblance of child's pose. About two minutes in, she borrowed the thermals off Visen again out of boredom. "Ooh there's a shoot-out in the southern stairwell."

"Yeah I saw that; I think they might need to borrow the thermal vision—"

"No, they'll be fine; Wheeler knows to call secret services, they always get things done faster; and they've got Ivle's prototype thermals too."

Ah.

By about ten minutes in, there were no more men, from either team, on this side of the mansion. Visen allowed herself to slide down the wall to sit next to Nadia. "We should stay here 'til they're done; just in case." There were still some combatants in the house's east wing.

Turned out, being a bodyguard was boring. Probably not as boring as being guarded. Visen smiled apology: she wanted to be out of there too; she wanted to see some action. But Nadia simply assumed Visen worried stuck-up practitioners of putting on nail polish didn't like spying out bad guys from secret hiding places.

"You know," she whispered, "this is actually really fun. It's probably really boring for you though, isn't it?" she only fully realized as she said it that she felt a twang of disappointment. "Have I been boring?"

"No, not at all!"

"You know, I really like you; you listen to me, and you know, let me do my thing—" Ivle never let Nadia slather him with antioxidants and exfoliants.

"I like you too,"

"How much?"

Oh. They were doing this now? It had changed from a whisper to breathiness, with the hint of a lip against

Visen's ear. They sat so close together Nadia's shoulder already overlapped Visen's arm.

"What do you mean?" she turned to find Nadia's lips close to her own. Nadia didn't need to answer. She could see the way Visen's eyes scanned her own now for any sign of a connection—that spark of liveliness Visen loved. Whenever that spark died out, and partner's eyes grew bedroom-lidded as though trying to prove they were serious, Visen always felt an instinctual tug of loneliness and fear, as though she ought to run. But the fire in Nadia's eyes remained playful, even now. In fact, it seemed to brighten, as the darkness fell past any need to speak; they were kissing.

So absolutely soft and silky, so perfectly inviting, that Visen's heart jumped even as the muscles round her pelvic floor lisped just a hint of a plea for more arousal.

"Do you like that?"

"Yes,"

Nadia pulled her closer, deepening the roll of fumbling, murmured hands, the faint lilt of lazy kisses lingering to unbutton each calloused demarcation of the tight-laced life Visen lived, as Nadia brushed her uniform aside, up and over her shoulders, pants away too.

Nadia'd wanted to do that ever since Visen'd been polite enough to listen to all her stupid stories over dinner, climax into pleasure the detached worldliness subtle enough to be bothered to laugh along with her when she was anxious.

Visen had already lifted Nadia's dress up and over her head, methodically, obliging, tweaking little snags away. Turns out the clasps on bras keep rolling sideways when you're trying to take them off someone else. Nadia, of course, managed to unclasp Visen's brazier with perfect ease, rounding the straps off her shoulders, hand curling down to smooth a palm against the peaked and breathing press of Visen's chest, as Visen kissed her neck, playing down the silken warmth of Nadia's inner thighs, cautious to sweep up and round, brushing closer, slowly, to the peaked thrill of gathered sensation, to see what she'd respond to.

"I'm afraid I don't know much—"

"Closer," Nadia pulled, nails suddenly taut against Visen's back, catching her left arm between them to guide Visen's fingers up and in, round the warmth of her drenched and rhythmic slide forward, teasing warmth.

"See? Just like you—" Visen could feel Nadia's nails slip the slightest play down the warmth of her own arching mount towards tightening in ecstasy— she pushed instinctively forward.

"I shoulda clipped my nails," Nadia whispered, "I don't wanna hurt you," God, even the way she undulated up against Visen's neck as she said it was sexy, head tossed back, a hint of lips against her ear.

"You're fine," Visen's voice came as barely a murmur through the lips she trailed down the subtly ribbed chest no longer half hidden by Nadia's plunging necklines— exploring the breasts hardened by surgery, their smallest of scars— tumbling down, as her hand explored upward, cautious, uncertain, as though hoping hands and lips could keep Nadia clasped in pleasure forever.

"Oh—" Nadia's pointed manicure dug suddenly at the taut cheeks above Visen's thighs as she moaned, clenching in time to the swipe and caress Visen played through the folds between her legs.

Now they both thrilled to feel one another, as they rolled over floorboards in the darkness.

Ack— Visen bumbled a bit too loudly against the baseboard that let out into Nadia's bathroom. For the first time she grew conscious of the fact fingering her boss' wife in a 3-by-6-foot box probably made a whole lot of noise.

"It's a bit tight isn't it?" she meant the room.

"Oh just—" Nadia wanted to say 'stay.' Visen stayed, at just the rhythm she'd played before, till they both fell into release, the warmth of Visen's own pleasure pressed in unconscious tilts against Nadia's thigh.

For a moment everything was still, as they lay curled on the cabinet's small floor, sleepy and dreaming of nothing.

Visen sat up first, realizing she'd been fogged in serotonin, to search apologetically for her phone, and see if they'd been missed— "It's okay, no one knows about this place except me,"

"I wanna—we need a larger space,"

"I need to trim my nails,"

Ugh, those were bedroom-lidded eyes and Visen still wanted to pound herself into orgasm just at the sight of them.

"Should probably see how Wheeler's doing," she was still too aroused to fully take in the fact she'd probably just made the biggest mistake of her career.

"You know, Ivle never does this with me; like, spontaneous?" Ivle never touched Nadia like that either.

Nadia wanted to do it again. She was still too breathlessly rosy to think anything beyond stupid little thoughts, like 'that was so much better than a neck massage; that was better than twenty neck massages!' but that was the most aroused she'd ever felt, the quickest, most demanding sudden arch that still encapsulated her whole body, and she had a feeling that'd only been the beginnings of what the arousal of being with Visen could offer.

Nadia didn't usually get off on penetration—she'd started into moaning in an attempt to rouse some sensation, as per her usual modus operandi— but now she definitely knew, for the first time from first-hand experience, that simply rubbing against her clit produced orgasms inherently not as strong, as the one she'd felt brewing at the touch of Visen's hand. That was something more. An instinctive arousal at being able to do this with Visen in particular. That was just— actually really— being physically aroused by someone.

"You wanna go again? For you this time?" she reached for Visen again, kissing down her torso's marbled muscles—

"Oh. —Oh no I haven't—shaved down there in ages—"

"I don't mind,"

"Nah —i-it's okay," oh no. The moment was gone now, a little bit.

Visen'd always felt self-conscious about her own lack of sexual grooming; there was just never any need—but the gleam in Nadia's eyes stayed just as tricksy as before.

"Brazilian waxing," she grinned, head cocked to a sexy side glance, like she could provide one, if Visen asked nicely.

"That really hurts doesn't it?"

"Torture training,"

"Haha—yeah…. Nadia?" Visen stumbled on trying to think. "Y'know, if anything ever does happen, I mean, you know, if they come. And Wheeler and I aren't here—or even if we are," she didn't know what she was trying to say.

"Aww! You caught feelings for me!"

"Ok, yeah no," Visen grinned like an over-acted hillbilly, rolling her eyes at herself to excuse the fact her protesting confirmed this was exactly what'd happened. "I just meant—" oh God, why did she have to be such a dork? What was she even trying to articulate? She had to grasp on to the remnants of SEAL training still flickering through her oxytocin-soaked mind. Alert. Attention!

"I was just thinking—" she noted the 'all clear' text from Wheeler on her phone.

"Mmhm?" Nadia curled a finger against her.

"Maybe it's—not the time—"

"No, no what is it?"

"No, I'm being a grandma."

"No! Did I do something wrong?"

"No—no that's just the thing you were perfect; without this place to hide— we might've died if this hadn't been here. I just—if something like this ever does happen again, I'm worried one bodyguard won't be enough. There were like 30 men out there! So even if— even if it seems like it might just be a repair guy— if it's not scheduled, till this is all over," (she wasn't quite sure what exactly 'this' was, but she meant whatever Ivle must be off taking care of now), "can you promise me you'll always have an exit strategy in mind? Plan an exit strategy for everything, even if, y'know, you're just getting your nails done."

"Oh my God, okay yes I will plan an exit strategy," Nadia grinned, rolling her eyes. Visen'd gone straight past grandma to ornery, concerned grandpa. "I don't actually know what that is though,"

"You don't— what?"

"An exit strategy?"

"Oh. How—? Like a way to get out,"

"Yeah, but how do you plan that there's just a door and then you leave, or you're stuck"

"No, I mean, in case there's someone blocking the door; you know,"

"You could train me?"

"Oh. Oh, yeah, that is a good idea; you should be trained in tactical maneuvers." Why hadn't Visen thought of that? Why hadn't Ivle thought of that?

"Ooh; really? Oh my God yes that sounds awesome!" Perfect way to excuse more cuddling (Nadia imagined 'tactical' as a cross between Judo and wrestling).

"Really?"

"Yeah!"

"Oh! Good!"

Visen had feared Nadia'd judge her worries for being lame. Because they were lame, a virginal, co-dependent, 'oh my God I could have killed this woman via negligent bodyguarding'—and then that enlightened climb of soul and trailing fingers—none of that, would have ever happened.

"Does training include kissing?"

"Lots of kissing,"

"Oh, gawd yes then I am ready for it! I wanna trim my nails," Nadia splayed her fingers out, cat-like, palms splayed gently against the soft perk of Visen's nipples and started thrumming the tips of her fingers against Visen's chest.

"Yeah… we should probably get out of here, right?" Visen could feel herself leaking against the floorboards; oh no, don't leak! That was so gross!

"Yeah okay yeah let's get out of here," now just talking with Visen gave Nadia the sense of a little thrill towards orgasm. She slipped back into her red dress, just as a pretense, in case anyone was in her room when they came out. Visen redonned her brazier, half unclasped, in the same motion by which she exited the towel cabinet.

"Should we go tell Wheeler we're okay?"

"I'll text; maybe we should have a shower first—"

"Oh God yes a shower! I'm gonna go trim my nails," *oh no*; had Nadia said that too many times? She'd never had sex with a woman before, one on one; she just wanted to keep Visen interested. Were short nails just some stupid ploy from porn she'd pegged on like some predefined lesbian? She was committed to it now though—she dived off to get her emery-board. Somehow little things made Nadia out of breath now, but in a pleasant way, like the muscles of her lower abdomen were saving themselves in taut suspension, anticipating what was to come.

"You guys?!"

"Wheeler! You little fucker! Why didn't you knock?"

"Hah! Ha ha ha—"

Visen didn't have a shirt on. Caught red handed, in nothing but a brazier. "—Ok sorry I'm going if you guys are good, I'm out of here—"

Maybe he'd misjudged; Visen looked so affronted.

"Why'd he give me that look?" it'd been a side-eyed 'I knew she'd get you too, eventually' look.

"Wheeler thinks I have sex with everyone," Nadia came over filing away varnish vindictively.

"Oh," Visen was obviously too polite to retort 'well do you?'

Honestly, first partner Nadia'd ever been able to characterize as someone who wouldn't do that.

"Which I don't!—sleep around—although for a while Evelle and I were poly," as in, Ivle started sleeping with other people almost as soon as they were married, so Nadia started sleeping with other people too, so she wouldn't devolve into a bitter mental breakdown, internalizing grudged hatred against her husband. Of course, she didn't *tell* Ivle about any of her affairs, which might seem counter-productive for revenge. But they helped her know her own sexual worth, you see, and that's what was important.

What Visen really wanted to ask was whether Nadia'd ever had sex with Wheeler, so she could guard against Wheeler telling Ivle they'd had sex by telling Wheeler she knew he'd had sex with Nadia too.

"Does that bother you if I've slept with a lot of different people?"

"No! Of course not!" Visen was a cool, calm, sexually liberated woman of the world. At least, she hoped desperately that's what she looked like to Nadia, instead of the dorky pre-teen hormonal puddle that finding herself virulently aroused for the first time in her life seemed to have turned her back into. Come on; six years of SEAL training; tough as guns. The sexy billionaire just wants a little fling, don't get attached—

Nadia got them out into the gardens for training in evasion tactics the next day. "Alright, so," she set out a picnic. "Are you gonna teach me something? Teach me how to maneuver like a sexy SEAL?" she reached for Visen almost instantly.

"Wait, right here out in the open?"

"What?"

"There's CCTV cameras on this side of the park," — private garden, whatever.

"Oh no it's just Wheeler; I can have him delete it afterwards,"

Somehow this gave Visen the impression they had in fact slept together before.

"Oh, I dunno Nadia—my job—"

"What? I do this with a lot of people, and Ivle never finds out. I mean—not like, the sex part with lots of people, well I mean sometimes the sex part—but never as good as our sex!"

"Thanks Nadia."

"No, I'm serious!"

"Let's—I don't wanna get fired—" This was the wife of the man Visen feared would execute her should she make one wrong move on covert deployments, let alone fuck his wife.

"Ok, ok, here; there's this *one* spot," Nadia'd spent ages analyzing Channel 2 precisely for an opportunity like this; she knew right where to go. It was an artificial grotto with waterfalls that had been sculpted to fall into specific patterns using a rare form of artisanal glass.

Oh. Ok.

"So. Teach me the ways of a Mertrian SEAL."

Right. So. Ahem. "The most important thing for you to learn first, is that you need to always have an exit strategy in mind, okay? So, if anything like—that—

whole—with the intruders thing— ever happens again, you don't wait for me, or y'know, whoever your bodyguard'll be, even if they're bogged down, your goal is to just get out of there, anyway you can; make that your top priority. Promise?"

Ok, this wasn't exactly what Nadia'd meant by 'teach me to be a sexy SEAL,' but—she gave attentive nods anyway.

"So, that means you should keep the thermal goggles with you. If something goes wrong, you check to make sure you have a clear line of escape; this goes for anywhere; wherever you stay, you memorize the layout. So, for this house, you can practice by memorizing the different ways you can get out, and then— where's your nearest neighbor?"

"Um. I think, about two miles south. That's where the village begins."

"Ok. Well, there'll always be someone in the cook's quarters—I guess,"

"Y'know, as long as there's still some sort of danger, Ivle'll keep you on as my bodyguard,"

"Don't you have a shifting rotation for bodyguards?"

"No, you're my first."

Ah hah! *Visen knew it!* So, she was being side-lined because she knew something she didn't know she knew. Either that or Visen was simply the least sexy bodyguard Ivle could provide for his wife. Good thing Visen'd fallen completely head over heels in love with her anyway….

"Well, I suppose we can always ask to keep me on, if there is a—"

"I'd like that,"

Their ten days were almost up.

"I'd like that too."

Funny, how Visen hadn't noticed she would miss this time, until now.

"You okay?"

"Oh, I'll just—miss this,"

"I'll get you rehired."

Something about the way she said it made Visen feel guilty, to think of Ivle as a husband, not a boss. Wasn't—entirely—his fault he saw Nadia as a Bentley—maybe? He had hired a bodyguard; he must love her somewhat, right?

"So, come on, fancy evasion tactics; we can delete the tapes afterwards, blame it on Desmond,"

And just in case Visen wasn't turned on by the thought of involuntary voyeurism, Nadia'd even thought to give Wheeler and his team a strategically timed unexpected day off.

They'd all known better than to question why.

Honestly, Wheeler assumed Visen'd been given the day off too and was just being stubbornly unresponsive when it came to disregarding her duty. He almost felt bad for Nadia, being unable to get rid of her— Visen'd done such a good job of playing asexual when they'd met up later to compare notes on the intruders.

Nadia slid trailing hands between Visen's breasts, slipping down beneath her bra to play gentle tweaks round her nipples as she listened. "So, what's the first evasion tactic, once I know the exits?"

"Sorry what was I—?"

"I go to the cook's?"

"Oh, right." Visen had to take a deep breath; get more oxygen to her brain. "Or the security guards' bullpin, although, since that's related to the main house you may come under attack there as well. So, try to get somewhere intruders wouldn't expect to find you, yeah?" Like the—hiding spot. "But don't show yourself. That's top priority. Keep low to the ground and shift—"

Visen enumerated what strategies they could practice, as Nadia straightened up a bit to pay attention. "Skirt around the edges of buildings, always try to have one side of you up against a wall,"

"—ooh that'd be fun to practice,"

"Yeah?"

"What else?"

Visen'd gotten lost in Nadia's eyes. "…and try to always think up at least three different ways you can outmaneuver someone, if they charge you." She tried to keep from slipping into kissing Nadia. Their lips had gotten awful close. "So, like, you know, don't box yourself in between three different walls—a bit like driving,"

"I don't drive,"

"Oh. Ok. Well."

"You could teach me how to drive?"

That actually would be a lot safer, if Nadia had two miles to go to reach the nearest friendly. But— "we only have two days?"

"There's a spare Bentley in the garage,"

"Oh,"

Nadia would never have thought she'd be interested in driving or maneuvers. But she loved the tactical exercises Visen knew, the way she could run them through her mind with precision, show Nadia ways to feint around trees, as though it were all a joke to get her closer so they could feel the press of one another once more, lip to lip, fingers twined, as they practiced sneaking round the pebbled garden slopes that had until that afternoon meant nothing but sheer boredom for Nadia's pragmatic burying of all her hopes for romance.

But this, this was lovely.

"You know Ivle's never even had sex with me outside?"

"Really?"

Visen, on the other hand, managed to incorporate trying to outrun one another, with herself as bogy hitman, into foreplay.

"So, ultimately, it's about seeing an opportunity, and taking it—" they bundled up against a tree breathing hard, "which, you'll be very good at; you always know just what you want,"

"Oh my God no that's not true I'm so indecisive!"

"Ok, just remember," Visen was having a hard time not laughing at being kissed in an abandonment proudly awkward at being able to transcend dorky self-consciousness, "underbrush doesn't conceal nearly as well as it should,"

"Yeah I got that one—"

"What else? If you're going down a valley, make sure to avoid loose stones or they'll—ack—" (*dies of pleasure—*) "they'll hear you! Stawwwp!"

Chapter 22

Ivle, meanwhile, continued towards the complete exoneration of convincing Badmonkof Livonia must have paid Colby to trick Smutt into thinking Ivle was behind some evil conspiracy. Unfortunately, Badmonkof was so moved by this turn of events he demanded another secret meeting—just Mertrian higher ups this time—to determine what steps Mertria ought to take in response. Not only was Ivle very disappointed to find Smutt among those invited, he was horrified that Badmonkof could think of no place safer to conduct such clandestine conversations than Ivle's own, Nadia-infested house.

"Sir, I have seven houses in the Pyrenes, perhaps we'd be better—"

"No, no I like going to your family home. Gives it a sense of comradery, you know, we're just in for a chat. Nothing serious. Plus, the Livonians know we're friends. They could mistake it for socializing. You could even bring your wife into the discussions; I'm sure she'd have valuable input from a feminine perspective."

Oh God no.

Ivle did bring in some higher ups from Swiverlia's federal ranks. To add a bit of gravitas, and, more importantly, the control he was seeking.

He arrived back home early and unannounced, the morning of the conference, to tie up any loose ends he might not want Badmonkof knowing about.

Visen was up early to do exercises while Nadia slept—a snoring bundle in silken sheets was far easier to keep an eye on while swapping out weights; it meant she only needed to keep an eye on her through the surveillance panel in her floor.

Ivle's knock at the bedroom door took her by surprise, but she took her gun and the towel she wiped sweat with and opened the door, looking flushed from 313 sit ups.

"Yes sir?"

God that was a slap in the face, after hoping to eat breakfast in bed with Nadia.

"I'll be coming back later this evening with a group of men; I need you to keep my wife away from them. Got it? I'm sure you've noticed by now she gets some pretty inaccurate ideas about what goes on around here, and it could do a lot of damage, were anyone to take her more seriously than she needs to be taken. Alright? Just— keep her on this side of the house. Understand?"

"Yes sir."

"I'll keep her phone's data off till this is all over."

"Yes sir."

"And then I'll call you when you can be relieved of duty."

"Yes sir."

Ivle hated how military Visen always was.

"Do you want me to go over what hap—"

"No, brief me later." What his wife had done for the last 10 days was hardly Ivle's greatest concern at the moment.

He texted Visen later to explain he'd be excusing Nadia's absence with claims she wasn't feeling well.

Visen watched as his helicopter touched back down late that afternoon, replete with dignitaries, while Nadia was bubbling in the solarium. It was easy to keep her from wanting to visit the dignitaries; Visen simply didn't mention dignitaries were visiting. Nadia didn't even notice her husband had come home; she didn't hear the chopper (all their mansion's windows were surprisingly soundproof).

From the fourth floor, Visen could see Ivle climb down from the helicopter first, beckoning for his buddy

Badmonkof, who followed him from within the confines of the Bell 237 with two additional VIPs at his heels. So, the Mertrian president was here… who else? Visen watched as administrative cars arrived next, pooling into their parking spots with such precise timing the last to arrive appeared five minutes after the first. Visen took out her binoculars. Heads of state poured out from behind tinted windows—Swiverlian and Mertrian. She could tell by the black military dress. But no Livonians.

They all trooped up the steps to a back door Ivle pretended was the front door in order to avoid Nadia's quarters, then up to a spacious conference room he used to discuss quarterly dividends with companies he didn't want to succeed. The chairs to the left of the huge shined-oak table were three inches shorter than the chairs to the right, a trick he'd learned from the KGB.

As soon as all the politicians had settled over cheese platters and wine, Ivle excused himself to call Visen.

"Alright. I'm back in residence."

"Nadia's safe. She's just practicing her bubble technique in the Solarium pool."

"Her—what? Never mind—not important,"

"Yes sir."

"Just keep her there. Good." Solarium was on the other side of the mansion.

Ivle re-entered the conference-room smugly. "Alright. I think we can all agree, someone in Livonia wants war. That's why they've tried to get me out of the way—"

"Or someone wants Livonia to look as though it's advocating for war."

One of the Swiverlian bureaucrats Ivle'd imported was actually a Livonian emigre who'd been unwisely picked for his post because he actually had Livonia's best interests at heart.

They'd been obligated to include him, because they wouldn't seem reasonable discussing Livonia if they didn't invite the one specialist on Livonia Swiverlian federal administration offered.

Everyone else around the room took to smiling very politely whenever he took to pointing out Livonia might not be to blame.

"Either way, it's clear we need to de-escalate,"

"Mertria doesn't want war—"

Their talks lasted late into the night….

~*~

About nine pm, Nadia finally noticed her husband was home.

"Oh, why didn't you tell me? I should have had dinner with him,"

"Uh—he's in a meeting actually; he told me not to bother you. It seemed a bit important; I don't think he'll be having dinner soon," (Ivle was currently surviving on whiskey, cigars, and cocaine).

"Here," Nadia flapped at Visen's shoulder, "lemme see your binoculars." She'd noticed the bureaucrats' cars.

Shit. Visen fidgeted warily as she watched Nadia rake zoomed-in vision across the little parked cavalcade that was so obviously trying to remain unobtrusive, over in a far corner of the estate. "Ooh, Badmonkof's here,"

"You memorized his license plate?"

All official Mertrian cars were the same make and color.

"No, but he never goes anywhere without Smutt anymore; and Smutt's is 021," she handed over the binoculars, "see?"

"Johann Smutt?"

"Probably? I dunno," Nadia trailed back round the couch behind them to flump into prime cube-matching slouch.

"Are you sure he's not just the liaison Mertria assigned to come to all meetings involving your husband?"

"Oh yeah, no, I've seen him out at parties with Badmonkof all the time— it's like a friend thing; galas, things like that; they go out to cafes together sometimes."

Since when had Nadia been spying on Badmonkof in cafes?

"What? I like Badmonkof; we hang out sometimes; he's the reason Ivle's so successful; I'm gonna text him and see if he's here—"

Appreciation of how very drastically this could have unhinged diplomacy, had Badmonkof not been invited, floored Visen with a new appreciation for Ivle's paranoia.

"Oh no yeah I'm—pretty sure Badmonkof is here, actually, I saw him get down from the helicopter with Ivle,"

"Awesome!" Didn't stop Nadia from texting. She continued to trail two-inch nails over her secret phone's much-abused touch screen, like a cat purring over a fishbowl.

"Whu—?"

"Well I wanna talk to him if he's here!"

Oh god.

~*~

Bwoop. Badmonkof's phone vibrated right out into the middle of the secret convocation's oval desk.

Badmonkof wasn't privy to technology's marvels enough to know he ought to silence his phone before meetings. (Mertrians had tried for three years now to tell him bringing phones to secret cabinet meetings could compromise security, but warnings hadn't worked. Eventually, they'd simply taken to removing the microphone from his phone before each conference instead.)

Badmonkof checked the phone's illuminated screen—not so slyly.

Swiverlia's Livonian representative had been arguing against Livonia's guilt for the past five minutes.

"Hmph," Badmonkof chuckled and put his phone back down again.

The room had just tensed towards a potential compromise that involved combining the two autonomous republics of Mertria and Livonia into one, if they continued to be unable to get along. But now everyone was trying to catch a glimpse of what Badmonkof had just found so funny.

"What I'm trying to say," the Livonian representative continued, perturbed, "is that Livonia's economy cannot compensate for Mertria's poverty!"

"So, what are we supposed to do instead? If Livonia builds up enough momentum to attack the Mertrians, they'll attack Swiverlia too,"

"Livonia's not pushing for independence; they don't want that!"

"No; they're waiting for revolution. Mertrian insurrections have given them ideas; they're not satisfied any more with Krakoveen!"

"Maybe because Krakoveen does such a spectacular job of shoving his head up his ass,"

~*~

"I wonder what they're talking about that's so important."

Badmonkof hadn't replied to Nadia's text.

"I think they're've been a few threats of Livonia going to war with Mertria," Visen was still analyzing how best to broach the fact if Ivle ever did find out about Nadia's secret phone, Visen'd be the one shot in the back of the head for it.

"But they're both autonomous provinces?" Republics—provinces—same thing. It meant they didn't have their own militaries, outside of the ones Swiverlia oversaw.

"Yeah, I think that's what makes it kind of weird,"

"Oh!" Badmonkof'd texted back. Nadia eyed Visen a moment. "You're not one of those jealous types, are you?"

"Mm, no I don't think so; not really; why?"

"Like we only had sex a few times and it doesn't even really count as sex the way I see it because we're both girls, right?"

Visen wasn't sure she liked the direction this conversation was going.

"Like, we're allowed to be more experimental with our sexuality, and that's what it is, like, an experiment, right?"

"Uh,"

"No like I really really enjoyed it and I wanna do it again and I'm trying to figure out a way to keep you around without boring you out of your mind, but like, you're not the jealous type right? That's just a thing some guys get all worked up about worrying over their alpha masculinity or whatever, but you know a few different sexual partners is healthy, right? Until you know for sure whose right for you, of course,"

"Yeah,"

Oh my God she was sleeping with Badmonkof.

"So, I wanted to show you some of these texts; look at these; isn't he sexy?"

"Oh. This is from your husband,"

"Huh? Oh no they're—" Nadia got up and turned off two security cameras Visen hadn't noticed before. "All the guys I sleep with are listed under Evelle's name in my phone, just in case; pretty clever right?"

—Ah, because then sexting wouldn't come across as anything out of the ordinary to anyone who noticed Nadia's phone buzz, except her husband.

How many guys were listed under Ivle's name in that phone?

"I mean like, he sleeps around with women every chance he can get, right? Like we all know wealthy marriages are different than regular marriages; I'm just covering my bases and making sure he gets promotions, y'know? Otherwise, like, why am I even here?"

"Yeah," Visen had never considered this side of international politics before, the horrifying, easily controlled whims of human nature she could, now she thought about it, readily believe were all too often behind the rise and fall of politicians' fortunes.

"So, can we do boy talk?"

"About Badmonkof?"

"Yah!"

"Ok! So. You're attracted to Badmonkof?" It seemed Visen's newly found self-confidence had been drastically premature.

"Oh, ew God no, he's really old; although he actually is really giving in bed,"

Visen hadn't had sex with anyone, outside of Nadia, in about three years, and even then, it'd only been a one-night stand. She tried to arrange her face into an appropriately 'oh that must be so nice' expression.

"So, look what he just sent,"

'*Missing your poise at this meeting; I'd love to see you tonight,*'

"Isn't that sweet?"

"Aw, yeah, that is really sweet," *Why did Visen feel crushed?*

'*I suggested they invite you but Ivle won't share,*' came next—plus a string of naughty emoticons.

"They have a Swinger's club in Swiverlian higher politics," Nadia explained.

"Oh." That was so much more than Visen had ever wanted to know about her terrifying boss' sex life.

"It's a really good way to overcome senate dead-locks, y'know? Providing everyone's consenting of course, but like, we're all pretty young so it's not like we're up to anything too gross; sometimes the older guys just sit around and watch,"

"I thought you said you'd never had sex with a girl before," That'd been one of the things they discussed when they ought to have been discussing tactical maneuvers.

"Oh, I haven't! Not like, one on one you know,"

Oh. *So that's why she'd been so good.*

"So, what do you think?" Nadia prepared to start texting again, "do you think I should invite him over tonight?"

"'ll I don't really know how long the meeting's gonna last," Visen wasn't even supposed to have told Nadia about the meeting. Though it was hardly her fault politicians'd parked in a way that was so obviously visible from the living room.

"Oh, they're all gonna stay over until like 5 am anyway; that's what they usually do,"

"This happens a lot?"

Visen wondered vaguely how many times Livonia and Mertria had almost been drawn into war.

"Oh yeah; Ivle always manages to fix everything with another one of his charities, ugh," Nadia mimed killing herself with a noose.

"Oh my God!" *Why was Visen laughing?* "Ok, so, well—ok, so you're gonna try to see Badmonkof around five," —analyzing the situation somehow helped it remain hypothetical. "Won't Ivle be coming back around then too?"

"Yess; can you help me with that?"

"Mm. Wait. So, Ivle's able to be so influential right now because," Visen flicked her pointer fingers back and forth between Nadia and an imaginary Badmonkof.

"Yeah; I mean also he's really good at his job but like that's not good enough in this line of work you know like you have to be able to offer something unique, you know? Like, he has other jobs in Swiverlia, but I like to think I definitely helped him out in Mertria, because otherwise why would Badmonkof be so interested in coming over to his house to discuss things all the time, y'know?"

Seriously?

"So uh, if you didn't meet up with Badmonkof, this time—"

"Oh, but we always meet up! Like he'll notice and think something's wrong," Nadia hadn't meant to be so coyly playful when asking Visen whether she should invite Badmonkof over. She'd just wanted Visen to feel power over Badmonkof's ability to sleep with her, so Visen would still be interested in her when she got back. But she actually probably really should still sleep with Badmonkof tonight, no matter what; that was kind of the arrangement….

"Ah."

Probably not the best time for Ivle's artificially won popularity amongst Mertrian politicians to take a nosedive, if he was already having enough of a political crisis to hold secret meetings and live in fear his wife would be kidnapped.

Visen calculated.

"Ok…. I'm just—a bit worried about the logistics of guarding you during that time, but yeah, I can, try to help—"

"Oh my god you're the best! Thank you! I'm gonna eat you out all Sunday!" Nadia jumped into a hug.

Oh Yay! Nadia thought Visen was the best!

The stupid little bit of Visen's brain that thought only in adrenaline and sex drives involuntarily flushed a warble of pleasure through her senses.

"You are staying Sunday, right?"

"Yeah I think so," that would be the tenth day.

"Good!"

"So, how are we—uh?" *Planning capacities completely and instantly gone.* "So, you want me to distract Ivle tonight, though, right?"

"Can you do that?"

Oh this was such a terrible idea.

But Visen didn't want to upset the status quo. Did she trust Nadia to read the situation correctly? Was sleeping with Badmonkof really all that necessary? Or was she just being played for a— dumbass. Hm….

"How? Do you want me to distract him?"

"I was hoping you could think something up?"

"Well." Visen supposed she could further debrief Ivle on the attackers who tried to kidnap his wife, though she was betting after a 17-hour session convincing Mertrians not to start a war, he'd be a little too tired for any updates other than the fact that they hadn't succeeded.

"Could Badmonkof just say he needed to go to bed early?"

"Oh! That's a great idea! Then we can see what Smutt gets up to when he's left on his own." Nadia texted, '*Hey Big Daddy*'

—internal screams from Visen—

'*wanna meet me at midnight to recharge?*'

It was now 10:30.

She texted again. '*I wanna see what Smutt gets up to when he doesn't have his hands tied.*' — "We don't trust Smutt," she explained— '*And I wanna see what you get up to when you ~do~*'

Bwoop

'**have your hands tied,*'

Bwo-op.

'*Did Ivle put you up to this?*'

Visen didn't like how automatically Badmonkof assumed baiting politicians couldn't be Nadia's idea.

'*No, I'm just trying to think up reasons you should come see me,*'

Hm.

Badmonkof actually *did* think it was a good idea to test whether Smutt could operate loyally on his own. (Badmonkof bet he could; Ivle was convinced he wouldn't—they'd been discussing it on the helicopter ride over). Maybe he could excuse himself, just for an hour or so, for an 'important call' he just had to take. Though how the hell had Nadia even known Smutt was here? Badmonkof glanced down the column of politicians beside him, so used to a general sense of mistrust it came now practically as an afterthought.

~*~

"So, if you do sleep with Badmonkof; do you get something in exchange, or, how exactly does that work?" Visen'd never been the best at analyzing politician's subtleties. She was trying to figure out how much, exactly, Ivle owed his wife's sexcapades. This couldn't possibly be one of the only things keeping peace between Mertria and Livonia—could it?

"O-oh. He brings presents sometimes," Nadia grinned. Badmonkof had a penchant for bestowing uncut diamonds on secret liaisons. Nadia was accumulating a collection in her safety deposit box down at the bank. She said a brother of hers sent them to her every blue moon, whenever Ivle asked about them.

"So—ok," Visen supposed sleeping with a grotesquely over-large geriatric patient was almost worth uncut diamonds that Nadia clearly would never actually get a chance to wear.

"Well it's not like I'm really attracted to anyone, when it comes to men. That's why I married for money; it's not fair if I don't get any pleasure out of it at all, so I might as well get something out of it I enjoy, otherwise what's the point in being alive, y'know?"

Visen didn't think this was the best moment to mention Nadia might have tried for a career, or some other, asexual pursuit, but either they were on the same wavelength or Nadia's chatter simply started down a likely trajectory of the current conversation: "I just never really found anything work related that gave me pleasure, y'know, like, I was never really good at math, and like science was cool but too many formulas—it was probably 'cause I was bored with sex; I've heard that's a thing. Anyway. —I've really enjoyed playing around with you, though; like, this is the most aroused I've ever been; you're so like—masculine, but like… not," she squinted as though overacting the hint that this was a mystery.

"Thank you," Visen had never been able to be that candid about her sexual preferences without instantly receiving definitive reaffirmation she was a creep. And she wasn't about to get used to expressing herself now. "I like you too, a lot."

"O-oh it's just so sexy the way stress makes your shoulders arch back a bit; I love it,"

The moment Nadia's words mixed with a slowly enunciating kiss, as she played up and into Visen's lips, instant relaxation released tension Visen hadn't even realized existed, bunched halfway up her neck. So, this was why Ivle was prepared to pay six billion in alimony just to keep Nadia around as a wife for a while.

The heady feel of Nadia's other hand slipping down to feel the curve of Visen's back brushed her into pure sensation as their bodies closed as one, clothes caught between—

But it was just a simple kiss. Simply— really well done.

"So, you're sure you're okay with me going to fuck an old guy now?"

"Yeah, sure," —*what was happening?*

"Ok so do you wanna help me pick out my outfit?"

"Is your husband gonna notice the cameras have been off this whole time?"

"I'll just tell him I was masturbating,"

"With me in the room?"

"No, I made you leave the room,"

"Okay."

"Ok; so, should we go for red lace? Or white lace? Or leather?"

About thirty extraordinarily tantalizing minutes later, Nadia was ready to slip back out into the hallway, looking perfectly ordinary, in her politely modern 'Kate Middleton may have worn this to Coventry' dress— if you didn't look closely enough to notice the odd bulges where lace rippled over her hips (the dress was, of course, unlike on Kate Middleton, conspicuously skin tight).

"You know," Visen paused, then finally took the plunge. "If Ivle's divorcing you, why do you want to help him increase his political standing?" the way she flinched, Nadia could tell she thought the question a bit too personal; the way it was enunciated was like a built-in apology for asking.

"Oh—well *I* don't wanna divorce him, remember? I was fine!" *Until I met you*— she realized. "Also, y'know, gotta make sure he keeps up enough power to pay off that alimony, right?"

Nadia realized even as she said it, she must be doing this slightly out of force of habit; not willing to antagonize Ivle any further with any off-beat questions Badmonkof may ask, were he to realize their routine was interrupted. "Alright, how do I look?"

"Wonderful. Should I... just stay outside the door then? Or—how do you wanna work this?"

"I'll just tell him I gave you the slip,"

"But—" Visen didn't want Nadia kidnapped. She also didn't want the Mertrian president to be told she'd fallen asleep on the job.

"Oh, I'll wink so he'll know I bribed you,"

That was somehow worse.

"Right, but, I do need to stand guard—"

"Oh, Badmonkof won't kidnap me,"

"Are you sure?"

"Yeah, he's the one whose gonna be tied up,"

Visen didn't quite understand how thrusting would work in that scenario, but she figured any anatomical uncertainly was probably just symptomatic of the fact she found women more attractive anyway.

"I'll stand at the end of the hallway, alright? If he knows you bribed me, he shouldn't have anything to worry about—reputation-wise; I'll look the other way when he comes,"

"Are you gonna use the heat goggles?

Ew no.

Oh God.

That might actually be necessary as a good way to ensure no hostile breaking and entry mid-coitus. Visen had a sudden stark realization of how very much she did not wish to have to burst in on the Mertrian president naked.

"You know that might be better—" Nadia liked the idea of thermals, "That way he won't feel like I'm having him spied on; he's kind of like—you know, self-conscious. You could maybe hold back and just follow us with the heat vision?" There were also security cameras; Visen had previously been content to leave Nadia under their transmitted, mechanical gaze — before, at least, the break-in that proved they could be easily turned off.

It just seemed like an awful good time for kidnappers to strike—a sort of, two for one deal, assuming Badmonkof wasn't about to let underlings know where he was headed.

"Okay, how about: I use the heat goggles until you're both in the room and Badmonkof can't see me, and then I'll come and stand guard down the hallway in case you need me, how is that?"

"Oh yeah no that works; although, I don't mind if you listen in; you can stand a little closer if you like; do you like that?"

"Not really; I just don't think it's a good idea to have the President all alone or you or—"

"Oh; this happens all the time! It'll be fine,"

Ehhhh... Did Nadia not realize Ivle could literally kill Visen, if anything bad happened?

"Ok, yeah that sounds fine; I'll," she tapped the thermal vision goggles, to let Nadia know she was ready to track her as she headed off.

"Ok, perfect! So, now you have to help me tell him how to get here," Probably best if Nadia went and retrieved Badmonkof from somewhere a bit more familiar to politicians who only frequented Ivle's east-wing shenanigans. Even Nadia didn't want Badmonkof to get lost all by himself, alone in their mansion.

She was also sensing a reluctance in Visen she chalked up to wanting to be more involved.

"Like, I wanna be sexy sounding, but like, also tell him how to get here,"

"He hasn't been to your room before?"

"Oh no never in this house; we usually meet on the Riviera," —Ah. Ivle's annual conference to discuss Mertrian military contracts with the President.

"Oh, right, ok…."

"Do you know what room they're meeting in?"

"No,"

"How about…" 'come out to the courtyard; I'll let you in the front gate'—gate quickly erased to become 'door'— 'gate' didn't have as sexy a ring to it. Or maybe it did—? It was technically a gate that led into the West Wing's atrium.

"Yeah that could work," As long as no one saw the Mertrian president sneaking to a sex scandal in such a highly visible location. "Or what about—um. Does he know where the hunting armory is?" Ivle had an entire room devoted solely to guns. And the way to get there from the day room they were in now was completely secure and closed off. That way Visen could feel relatively at ease about Nadia, at least.

"Yeah! Ok; good thought," Nadia sizzled back into the sexy little wriggle with which she texted all sensuous messages, to get a feel for the voice she'd be using if she were talking out loud.

'*Meet me at the armory*' "…Hm." Didn't have quite as nice a ring to it.

Visen just knew if she were the one texting, she'd add something like 'you sexy beast' and instantly ruin things. She wasn't very good at sexting. Or flirting. Or subtlety, really, now that she thought about it.

'*I'll be waiting for you*' sly-face emoticon.

"Yeah that sounds sexy," —mainly because Visen enjoyed imagining Nadia being sly.

"Ok good." Sendsies. "So, like, this is okay with you?" Nadia turned, nervously nodding, just one more time to make absolutely sure.

"Oh— yeah, of course!" They'd slept together one night; fiddled around a few days. That gave Visen no right to worry Nadia about her private affairs. Memories of Colby hitting on her whenever she tried to do anything flashed through her head.

"Oh my God dating girls is the best! Not that we're dating. But we have been hanging out for like —what? nine days right? and we had sex—kind of? —on three of them—oh my God am I forcing you into things?"

"No, no. I like—having relations with you," why was stringing of words together so difficult right now?

"Oh my God; such a sergeant; ok I'm going; wish me luck; are *you* interested in being tied up?" Nadia turned back as an excited afterthought.

"Not really,"

"Got it!"

She blew a kiss goodbye.

Chapter 23

Then, as soon as she was out in the corridor—Visen having sat down a moment to turn on the heat goggles and gather her thoughts—Nadia started texting Badmonkof to meet in the bedroom she usually slept in when Ivle wasn't out of town, instead of the armory. That subsidiary bedroom was where she and Badmonkof usually met, she'd just really been trying to downplay the whole 'sleeping with Badmonkof a lot' thing, so Visen wouldn't feel jealous—and so Visen would feel as though spending time together sexually for three days in a row was a really big deal, because it was: Nadia'd loved every minute of it; she just hadn't known Visen for as long as she'd known Badmonkof—but she didn't want to admit greater intimacy and accidentally break Visen's heart. Stoic people were so secretly sensitive; Nadia was always worried about them.

Her subsidiary bedroom, for staying out of Ivle's way when she could guess he was probably going to come home roaring drunk with a mistress, stood halfway down a gorgeous hall lined with plushy red things: plushy Persian carpeting, plushy red wainscoting—this was the 'Louis XIV couture' section of the house, designed by Ivle's third wife, which he kept around, despite frequent redecorating, as a nice way to impress cabinet members from out of state. They were usually given sleeping accommodations in this wing, on the third floor, past which Badmonkof now ascended as sneakily as 350 pounds can sneak.

He'd told all the other politicians he had a pressing matter to discuss with his Minister of Defense (the Ministry of Defense had not, of course, been invited to their discussions as to whether or not they should start a war), and everyone else adopted the subconscious assumption it must've been this minister who'd sent the texts Badmonkof found so funny. Badmonkof wasn't president of Mertria for nothing; he knew how to play politicians.

He also knew the path to Nadia's Louis XIV bedroom very well. To get there, he had to walk down a hallway that had been completely darkened by disuse for the past 10 days, relying on nothing but moonlight, which gave the shadows an ethereal lurkiness, as though something altered about reality played just round their edges.

Visen was just braving the thermal goggles to find Nadia had in fact either given her the slip or actually been kidnapped, when a loud screech alerted her to the fact that she ought to be directing her gaze towards the section of Ivle's house that jutted out across the lawn, where, indeed, two blobs of thermal heat could be seen on the fourth floor, one of them rapidly cooling.

Instant floodlights compromised the location of Ivle's secret conference by proving it must have taken place somewhere up the mansion's South-East stairwell, as five men came spilling out that side door in an attempt to locate the scream, followed by fifteen more who felt awkward just sitting and waiting for someone else to tell them what had happened, when so disconcerting a sound occurred on private premises.

Visen got to Nadia first. She could run much faster than middle-aged politicians weighted down by 6 hours, already, of interminable dangling arguments.

Badmonkof had been slashed across the neck, and Nadia was crying. "What happened?"

"Vi-i-isen?"

Ah fuck it. No one else was even in sight yet. She bundled Nadia's shaking bare back into the warmest hug she could manage, trying to comfort her around the confines of having forgotten to take off the thermal glasses. Stupid—head gear.

"Are you okay?" On second thought, thermals back on; area scanned: no one in sight.

"He was just—lying there!"

Nadia couldn't actually have killed someone, could she? The thought occurred as Visen was still hugging her: death must have taken place in the first few seconds Nadia's misdirection disoriented Visen; Badmonkof's pulse was gone, but his wrist was still very warm.

Now the running politicians arrived; Ivle almost in the lead. "What happened? Did you let her out of your sight?"

Oh, Ivle knew all about what was going on between Badmonkof and Nadia. Stupid slut. She flirted with him non-stop. After all Ivle'd done to climb to his position of power—to be undercut by a woman who could think of nothing but the pleasures of sex for a few diamonds. (He knew about the diamonds too).

"No; she was showing me the tapestries."

"You both found him?"

"Yes."

Thank God Visen was a fast runner.

"What happened?"

"He just—had his throat cut,"

"What?"

Politicians crowded round.

"There was no one in the hallway when we came,"

"Had his throat cut," the politicians relayed back to one another.

"By what?" a few politicians at the back pressed forward.

"By this, I'm assuming," Visen held up a clump of dark netting she'd found to one side. It was tactical gear, quite out of keeping with the Louis XIV vibe: meshy encasement enough to enclose a body and affixed to a wire presumably intended to whip it across the corridor in time to envelope whoever happened to be walking by.

Badmonkof's circumference must have thrown off whatever delicate scale tripped the wire. Visen followed its chord back with her fingers to where it slipped through a hole in the wall's wooden paneling. From the size of the bag, it was probably meant to fit round Nadia. What the fuck kind of kidnapping attempt was that?

"Do you know what it is?"

"No. Not really. But I think this might've been an accident." Visen could see blood on the thin wire chord attached to the bag.

Badmonkof was about 200 pounds heavier than Nadia. That meant the weighted trigger had been let off by over double the intended stimulus, which would have set it racing out across the hall much faster than planned. At that unforeseen speed, the wire was sharp enough to cut a neck five inches above where it was expected to be.

Visen explained.

"So, you've seen this sort of thing before?" The politicians huddled, very impressed.

"No, I'm just guessing," she knew as much about kidnapping trophy wives as they did—come to think of it, potentially less. All she did was shoot people from 50 meters away.

"Could it have been for one of us, then? Is that what you're saying?"

"No," not necessarily.

"But who on earth would want to kill Badmonkof?"

Visen thought she'd just made that clear—it was probably an accident. She reiterated the fact that the bag did not, in fact, look like it was meant to kill anyone,

"So, did Badmonkof try to kidnap her?" Someone pointed at Nadia, having noticed the fact Visen had discretely tried to avoid: the bag *was* just about the right size to envelop Nadia completely.

"No, I don't—think so?" Visen took her cues from Nadia's vehemently shaking head. Everyone else seemed to overlook the realization they might be able to question Nadia directly.

To be fair, Badmonkof did usually blunder when it came to using technology....

"Wait—I think he's still alive!" someone had bothered to check the President's pulse again. They had read it very, very wrong. "Oh no wait."

"Maybe if we—" Nadia tried to make things better by kneeling gently beside Badmonkof's prone form and pushing his head down so as to align it back up against the rest of his neck.

"Badmonkof?"

Politicians seemed to have a very poor understanding of basic human anatomy.

"We should call a doctor—"

"No! Wait! We can't let this get out!" Badmonkof was the Mertrian President for Christ's sake; even if he had been elected by rigged elections.

"Well I dunno what else we're gonna do—"

"We should call the police."

"Sir?" Visen motioned Ivle aside with a nod towards the stairwell. "I think this may have been set by the intruders who broke in about three days ago,"

"What—? The—? Why didn't you tell me this?"

"You said to debrief you later. —I didn't get a good look at them, but they weren't wearing insignia corresponding to any modern militia; they were free agents, I think. Wheeler brought one into custody down at the local police station; they should be able to tell us more. They promised to email you a debriefing."

"I didn't get a debriefing."

"Then I'll call the local sheriff, see what's taking so long,"

"No, call Wheeler."

Wheeler reported, once the phone had been handed over to Ivle, exactly as Visen had claimed he would: the one suspect his men caught had been taken off his hands by the local constabulary. The local constabulary, subsequently called, claimed they'd had nothing substantive enough with which to hold the young man, and had had to let him go.

"I'm calling Fetchins," Ivle stormed off. Fetchins was the Secret Service task force head Wheeler had called for help, who ought to have known better than to rely on inept local constabulary when Swiverlian officials were involved.

"Think he could be a little more concerned," one politician snidled to another, "it is his house-guest." The rest were half-wincing, half-crouched, round the body, rapidly reading what sort of mood they might be able to pick up from everyone else.

"Let's get him put in the nearest bed, or couch—" Visen decided.

"But all that blood!" This was Nadia. No one else had responded.

Visen ducked down beside the still-crouching pulse-taker. It was Smutt.

Johann Smutt.

So, the Smutt Nadia said followed Badmonkof around everywhere *was* the Smutt with potentially damning evidence against Ivle, if Colby had talked fast enough. What did that mean? What was Ivle playing at, inviting him over? He was wary of this man, wasn't he?

"I thought you said he was still alive."

"Well I—might've been wrong about that—"

"Lemme see," no pulse. But this lot weren't about to help Visen move the body; and she had a bad feeling they weren't going to allow an inquest. "There is a little something there," she lied. Now they were obligated to help.

They left Badmonkof on a settee and raced back to analyzing how best to bring in medics. Back entrance, definitely, so civilians wouldn't see which members of Swiverlian bureaucracy were parked outside.

"Oh, come on, they won't be able to tell from cars— It's not like anybody bothers to memorize license plates!"

Nadia went to go get Badmonkof a glass of water. "Are you doing okay?" Visen drew her aside.

"Yeah; I'm okay; a lot of the old ones go with strokes and stuff pretty unexpectedly, and—maybe he'll pull through,"

A lot of the— what?

"—Nadia," Visen whispered that she'd lied.

"Oh."

"Try to keep them thinking he's alive though; if we can have an outside witness it might be helpful," she didn't trust politicians; she'd worked for too many of them.

At least blood marked where Badmonkof had fallen. It could open investigations, at the very least, into who precisely had set up that trap.

Nadia nodded. "Alright, I'm on it." She bustled round to Badmonkof's side with the cup of water she'd brought in, to feed sips of it delicately between his lips.

"You want a little bit of water? Little water?"

Oh God Nadia, too much.

Water dribbled off to one side, but everyone else assumed Badmonkof'd swallowed some. Oh good. There went a fixed time of death.

No one really wanted to call a doctor, though; they kept putting it off by deciding they should wait till Ivle returned from yelling at Fetchins. No one really wanted outside witnesses knowing they'd held a top-secret conference of Mertrians and Swiverlians without telling Livonia.

Apparently, though, while talking with Fetchins, Ivle must have mentioned Badmonkof had just been shivved to death by a metal string, because about twenty minutes later Fetchins himself came flying over to confirm time of death in detail, despite Nadia's attempts to be hospitable by subsequently fetching Badmonkof's body a warm face cloth.

Visen supposed Fetchins would have to do, as far as documenting the incident was concerned. Fetchin's small skeleton crew for discreet dealings would arrive at six in the morning to collect the body.

In the meantime, he closed them all into an antechamber just beside Badmonkof's settee to impress upon them: "No one. And I mean no one. Is to know about this for now. Alright?"

If word got out that Mertria's president had been killed under suspicious circumstances, before police had time to examine the evidence—which Fetchin's crew even now was doctoring to avoid letting the world know Ivle's wife had been the victim of an attempted abduction (bad publicity, that)—Livonia would be blamed, war would be required, and Nadia's would-be kidnappers would know they needed to set another trap.

The ability to hide that little detail from other politicians flew out the window as soon as Fetchins started questioning whether Ivle could have been responsible for the contraption.

"Ahm," Visen stepped up to verify. "We think intruders last Friday may've planted the mechanism—"

"I don't understand though; why are they trying to kidnap Nadia?"

Several of the other politicians were sleeping with her too, you know.

"Leverage, they want leverage over the negotiations," Ivle reassured.

"Presumably they've been hiding out, checking periodically to see if the trap has been triggered, and then when they see it has been, they —just come and collect her, I guess?"

"How would they—know she'd been enveloped, though?" Without, y'know, sneaking back in periodically to see if their mesh bag on the fourth floor had caught anything human-shaped.

"The Livonians!" Ivle realized. "I just sold them thermal finders! They could check using thermals!"

"It's not the Livonians!" the Livonian expert was obviously getting very tired of using this phrase.

"It better not be, my friend,"

"Whoever it was probably hacked your surveillance feed; that'd be simplest to do, and not very hard."

"Which means they've already seen all this has taken place!"

"Unless. They don't review the tapes in real time—"

Technical experts were called in to scan the house for bugs in amongst the wires of Ivle's pristine CCTV recording systems.

"We did check that routinely, sir—"

"People—people!" Fetchins was still trying to create order. In the end, his crew funneled all political staff into Ivle's not-so-secret, secondary, unlocked office —

which ended up being an enormous task as every pen-pusher seemed to have brought his own adjunct. It wasn't just the people Ivle'd invited to argue over war in his conference room. It was also all their personal assistants, PR representatives, and policy consultants.

"Ok we just cannot, at this time, analyze exactly what has gone on here; so, I want no one to jump to rash conclusions, please just remain in this room; this may simply have been an accidental death—" Fetchins' own PR consultant had somehow found a podium to stand behind. They had at least confirmed by now that Badmonkof was officially dead.

"Sir? There's no bugs in the wires!"

"Then how the fuck would they know when to—?"

Ivle just faded off, scowling at the bungling mess everyone seemed to be making of things, until he became aware, gradually, that he was listening through the wall to a very excitedly hystrionic Nadia explaining to her sister what all had just happened; "Ohmygod Marge you won't believe it; I think they've just up and killed him!"—Her sister lived in Conneticut—

"Oh no wait! Nadia!" he wrenched open the door and managed to grapple her phone away in time.

"What?!" she flummoxed, "what the hell?"

"What the hell is this?"

"It's a phone!"

He wasn't about to admit he'd denied his wife cellular service in front of notable dignitaries. "Ok—we can't let other people know about this right now, okay? Weren't you listening?"

"Are you crazy! They're gonna come get him anyway! —Aren't they?"

"Wha—? Yes! In private! Not for some rubber-necking—"

"Don't you call my—"

"We're too close to war! —You understand?"

Had he hung up on her sister? He checked. He'd hung up on her sister.

"You can't just—"

"I don't want a dead body just hanging out in my house! There are bloodstains in my bedroom!"

"That's not your bedroom,"

"It's a spare bedroom!"

"Ok, Nadia, that's not—" They were never actually supposed to go to war! This was all just power balancing, not courting Armageddon! "This is more important—! This is a very sensitive situation, we can't just let the public know—!"

"What? Is this that stupid Mertria-Livonia thing again?"

How did she always know about top secret complications?

Ivle tried to make a noncommittal 'yeah? Maybe? shut up?' growl by only shrugging with his hands and raising half a lip suggestively.

"Well maybe they did it—maybe the Livonians killed him!" Nadia pointed. The Livonian expert from Swiverlia had just walked through the door, with his traditionally Livonian mustache.

"No! No of course they didn't! Livonians fight fair; we're all civilized here—"

"Well you're the one who—"

"Shut up!"

"Who did what?"

"I don't know! She has crazy ideas I don't like the Livonians because my fifth brother in law was from there—Visen! Get her out of here! Now!" Ah. There it was. Ivle really did get 'fumey'.

"Yes sir; right away; come on," Visen motioned with the same nod she'd used to step Ivle aside, only, somehow, slightly more sympathetically. Oh, great this was just what Ivle needed; a fucking softy of a sniper taking sides with his wife. He glared at the two of them until they'd left the room.

"What ah— but—but wait!" Nadia turned back round, "are they gonna take the fucking body?" She hadn't been listening to Fetchin's debriefing, "are we gonna be stuck with a fucking body for a week?"

"We know how to dispose of a body Nadia!" Again, not sounding so great, PR-wise. What was it about his wives that permanently fucked with Ivle's brain right when he needed to play it cool? They were just so… so stupid. It was like they rubbed off on him. That was it. Had to be. The stupidity was somehow catching.

He could hear Nadia chattering down the hall: "but are they gonna take the settee too?"

It was like peering into an entirely other world, that ran parallel, but separate to Ivle's own, with entirely difference nuances and cares. Sometimes the two worlds would look in at one another, across the divide of differing perception, but neither ever really understood what they saw on the other side, even if they were speaking the same language. Odd, how 'foreign' was a set of expectations, not vocabulary or a border crossing. And Ivle's wife was the most foreign representative in that entire house.

Chapter 24

Nadia had, luckily, taken the ability to dispose of a body as some sort of threat, and disappeared accordingly.

"Alright, let's, regroup; figure out what to do," it was the only way Visen could calm herself as she poured Nadia whiskey, back in the bedroom Ivle knew about, in the house's west wing.

"Do you think Ivle killed him? Do you think he found out about us?"

"No; I don't think he was meant to die. I just don't understand—" what Nadia'd been doing on the fourth floor in the first place, when she'd told Visen she'd be meeting Badmonkof in the armory.

There wasn't a room on the fourth floor that looked even remotely like an armory, so it wasn't exactly like Badmonkof could've gotten confused.

And if Nadia planned to lie about where she was going in the first place, why bother to ask Visen for suggestions as to where she could meet Badmonkof? Purposeful misdirection? Visen's overly military mind would never have thought it possible someone could engineer an entire deceit for the sole purpose of accommodating another person's emotions. Should she just ask Nadia to explain herself, outright? …But something held her back. She should test this, somehow; see if Ivle was right to worry—

"So, the room Badmonkof was found outside—is that room used a lot?"

Nadia, for her part, simply assumed Visen would accept she and Badmonkof had switched locations, without bothering to question why. That sort of kerfuffle always happened on trysts—God, it happened just going out to dinner. (Visen wouldn't know, she didn't have any friends).

"Yeah, I use that room to meet up with people sometimes, like, I usually meet Jacobsan there to go over questions about the divorce,"

"—When you? Ok, how often?"

"Um, I think we were gonna try for next Monday; I dunno, we hadn't really ironed it out,"

"Did you text him about those questions, already, by any chance?"

And did those questions, if already texted, involve expounding on presumptions Ivle secreted illegal documents and forged proofs of nuclear reactors?

"Yeah, I mean we were just texting back and forth—with the—"

Right. With the secret phone.

"But it couldn't be Jacobsan behind this; he knows he can't get any leverage over Ivle through me; he knows we're divorcing,"

"Well—"

"I mean, so, I'd lie if I could, right? So, testimonial's spotty coming from me unless it's civilian court y'know what I mean? And I'm assuming if it's kidnapping, they're not just trying to get at me like over the divorce thing,"

"Well, right, I mean— So, you're saying whoever wants to kidnap you likely doesn't know you and Ivle are divorcing?"

"Yeah, I guess; maybe? But I'm more just saying I do go in that room a lot, to meet people."

She also went there to meet up for sex a lot. Usually for sex, really.

"Ivle doesn't think I like going in there 'cause his third wife furbished it, so it's perfect,"

"Oh." Visen looked like she was still stuck on the routinely-meeting-up-for-sex thing. "Isn't Jacobsan Ivle's lawyer?"

"Yeah?"

"So, if you're, trying to divorce—"

"No, no I don't want to divorce; Ivle's the one who was gonna go through with it, remember?"

"Yeah," but, didn't that still require Nadia to have her own lawyer…? "Alright. So, who else could've known to lure you to meet them there?"

"Ooh." Nadia hadn't thought to summarize it so succinctly.

Of course, as far as Visen was concerned, that mantrap couldn't be anything other than a lure: text Nadia to meet up, then boom! Bagged.

Whoever'd managed to get 17 people past Ivle's security knew far more than even abusing access to Swiverlian secret service records had taught Desmond. They knew codes; they knew floor plans. And the only way to know more than secret services in a police state was to be a closely trusted friend. In this case, a friend who knew Nadia routinely met up for sex in the east wing.

"So, anyone in the Swinger's network you mean?"

"…Yes?"

This turned out to be literally every single one of their 'family friends'. For friends, it seemed Nadia had a choice between Ivle's various defense-contractor colleagues, all of whom were male and over 40, and Ivle's secret service contacts, all of whom were male and over 60. No wonder Nadia had no choice but to interpret them all as 'friendly'. One would go mad otherwise. Visen began to realize why she'd been so excited to be able to have a 'girl's only weekend' with her bodyguard.

Luckily, her phone listed, in the notes section for each contact, the actual name of whoever was sending her sexualized emoticons as 'Evelle'.

Let's see… that was, the cook, 3 gardeners, every single lawyer Ivle had ever hired—no wonder Jacobsan was being so helpful about the divorce—2 Mertrian senators, 4 Livonian cabinet members, a duke (origin unknown) ("I'm especially proud of that one," Nadia thumbs-upped as soon as she realized Visen wasn't flying off the handle, the way Ivle would)—two Turkish ambassadors, "who honestly seemed more interested in one another," a ferry man ("I went to Shetland once!"), a soldier from Afghanistan, Colby, 2 French men, and an electrician named Marcos.

She smiled up at Visen, half hopeful half nervous when they were done. "Are you mad at me?"

"No, that's—really impressive." Must support sexual progressivism, instead of being secretly heartbroken at finding herself just another link in a chain.

"I always check for STDs too; I don't have any; don't worry,"

"Nice, no I— trust you. It's a good start to go on, though, 's good," Visen studied the listed names again unnecessarily.

"You want me to tell you who I think it could be?"

"Um. I should probably do some background checks on them all first,"

"Ok. Do you want me to help?"

"No that's okay; I'll just be upstairs, though, okay? Just— holler if you need me, although— it'd probably? be best if you stayed in here until I get back, I'll keep the CCTV monitor on you," electricians *had* just proven the security system bug free. "Is that okay?"

Leaving Nadia in her main bedroom, of course, meant Visen had to ensure extra hard she didn't sniffle too loudly when she got upstairs, because the surveillance panel was still open between the two rooms.

It was only one sniffle! It was more banging her head down softly next to the computer's keyboard in utter embarrassment at the thought that having sex with Nadia had meant so much to her, when it was so very clearly just another weekend excursion for Nadia.

It was just— Visen was always such a failure, wasn't she? First her career completely derailed by blackmail, despite having sacrificed everything to get to the top. Now she'd fallen in love with a housewife who was so clearly above her in every way. And she hadn't even realized how much she did like Nadia until now. Full of— perky idiosyncrasies, matter-of-fact madness. She really did feel the beginnings of love for that stupid Brooklyn floozie —and now, she'd be leaving, and Nadia would forget all about her.

Ah, well, c'est la vie.

Why was she upset by this, and not the three nonentities she'd had to personally kill in the line of duty for Ivle's OPSAI, blindly trusting they'd deserved the bullet through their brains? She hadn't even cried when her career had been completely derailed.

Maybe because this was so small and stupid. She expected everything else in the world to go wrong. She didn't expect a single long-nailed housewife from Brooklyn to be far less desperate and more successful than she was, even if only in matters of love. Which was of course, ridiculous; she ought to have expected exactly that. Maybe that's why it hurt so bad.

Nadia went back to stacking cubes, with a vague sense something was off, which she made herself promise (to herself) that she wouldn't worry about until more definitive proof of something wrong presented itself.

~*~

Meanwhile, the politicians were forming into cliques. The way power was transferred in Swiverlian autonomous republics, every single bureaucrat in the room had a chance to succeed Badmonkof in his— if not lucrative— well-positioned post as President of Mertria.

A council of nine would decide who became Mertria's Interim President. Accepting the post was seen as a great and sacrificial honor, mainly because interim presidents had a habit of being bumped off in the same way their predecessor had unexpectedly departed.

In truth, the slow inefficiency leant Swiverlian bureaucracy by their determination to govern 18 autonomous republics simultaneously, meant Mertria's interim president would serve in his post— if he survived— for at least another four years before Swiverlia got around to organizing re-elections for his replacement— (the Republics weren't, after all, that autonomous)— which was plenty of time to ensure the elections could be rigged in the presiding interim president's favor. The opportunity, therefore, potentially meant president for life.

"I think we should alert his wife,"

"Right! Yes," Badmonkof's wife was very popular with city-dwellers in Swiverlia. Perhaps photos of Ivle with his arm around her while she grieved would prompt someone to mention to their elder relative in politics how perfectly under control Ivle kept everything. He did reside in Mertria… (at least during the summer months) —that was one of the requirements for becoming Mertria's interim president.

"I think Krakoveen ought to be informed too," Smutt, personally, thought Krakoveen was the killer. But he was hoping to form a stronger alliance with

Livonia this way. Mertria could use an interim president with strong ties to Livonia right about now....

Chapter 25

Visen returned to Nadia's room about 3 hours later, having run background checks on all 52 names from her phone. It was awkward knowing some of the lawyers in attendance on Ivle at this very moment owed 200 billion dollars' worth of back-taxes for offshore accounts Ivle was hiding for them.

"Alright. I think our best bet might be the political consultants from France; our visitor in the library was wearing slightly dated French tactical gear, he may have come into politics through the military, and never bothered to get rid of his old kit."

"He seemed a lot younger than my Frenchmen though," they'd both been upwards of 85.

"Serious—?" Ok. No need to question. Viagra was a powerful drug. "Valid point." The intruder they'd seen did step far more lithely than a 85-year-old could.

"Visen…" Nadia'd been thinking. "Whenever Badmonkof does politics he carries a little suitcase with him; it wasn't in the hall, so it'll still be in his room, or in whatever room they were meeting in,"

"Ok."

"It's got the lists Desmond keeps trying to steal in it."

"How do you know?"

"Ivle brings his lists to conferences too, in case he needs to convince someone to do something. There's like 2,000 people on there each month; they can usually find a cousin or something,"

"Ok. So, you're thinking whoever did this, might have wanted the list?" Visen thought she'd done a good job establishing the mechanism hadn't actually been meant to kill Badmonkof.

"No, I'm thinking if I give Desmond the list, he'll stop cutting the lights off every Thursday."

"Oh. But if it's a monthly list—"

"I mean they're not really good at keeping records. If whoever he wants off that list has been on it for the past three months, they're not that high up priority-wise. They probably won't bother putting them back on. Like, if it was just for ordering something from the United States or something, they've probably already lost all the evidence by now anyway."

"Oh."

"Do you mind getting it for me? Or do you think I could go and get it? I just texted Audrey and told her I'd do it," Audrey was Desmond's wife (nicknamed Nori).

"Ah…" Ok, international incident impending. Awesome.

"You don't think it's a good idea?"

"Not really,"

"But I already told her I'd do it,"

"Ehhh…"

Visen's old suspicion Nadia'd let Desmond go on purpose resurfaced. Could Nadia have killed Badmonkof for the list? Would leave her short one supply of uncut diamonds….

"What are you going to do with it, if you do get it?"

"I'll just burn it I guess, and then tell Nori I did of course," They only had fake electric fireplaces in the house, but Nadia still smoked in secret; she'd never kicked the habit.

"Ok."

Maybe seeing who all was on that list could show Visen whether Nadia found it worth killing for. Could she memorize all the names fast enough to do a background check on all of them as well? What was Nadia's maiden name…?

"Yeah I guess we can— try to get it,"

"Oh, good okay! If we get Badmonkof's copy now, I can get Ivle's copy later. And then we won't have to worry anymore, because Ivle and Badmonkof are the only two holders for Mertria; Badmonkof told me," And the lists were top secret enough they didn't have digital backups, because anyone high enough in government to know they were compiled would never like evidence they existed to ever be found.

"Oh okay." That meant they weren't legal. "Let's— alright." Visen reached for the thermal googles and adjusted them against her eyes to scan the east wing. All the politicians were still huddled near the room they'd moved Badmonkof into.

"Do you know where their conference room was?"

"No. I don't really go into that part of the house that often, except for—y'know. But it can't be that hard to find, right?"

"Yeah, okay." It was just tampering with evidence.

What if Desmond had killed Badmonkof? Anything was possible; what if he'd worked out a way to get inside? What if Wheeler'd fucked up the breaker box in some drastic way Visen'd never noticed? Oh God, then it'd be her fault. She ought never to have been left alone to guard an entire manor house; she wasn't good at multitasking; this sort of thing required such omnipresent subtlety to the way one focused. She was sure Ivle'd just assumed she could do it because that's how everyone always assumed women naturally focused—on 10,000 things at once, if ridiculously complex cooking instructions were anything to go by— well not Visen; now Ivle'd just assume she couldn't do anything right at all. Brilliant.

She watched via thermal vision as a contingent of 5 politicians made their way to the backdoor to welcome Badmonkof's wife. Her chauffeur had been instructed, under pain of death, not to take her round the front way, just in case Galice did know any of their license plate numbers by heart. No use adding to the list of people who could enumerate who all had been there that night; it was supposed to have been a secret meeting, after all.

Visen and Nadia slunk down an adjacent stairwell, as soon as the contingent welcoming Galice passed by.

Alright, the politicians had run to Nadia's aid from the direction of the South-East stairwell. That meant the conference room had to be in the south half of the house's East wing. Great. That was four floors to search.

They were looking for hastily disturbed detritus of notepads, laminated reports, and whiskey. Honestly that wouldn't actually be too hard to find. Especially when Visen turned on her thermal-vision goggles to find a lone figure hastily ransacking a room two stories above them. "Ahah." She pulled out her gun. That had to be the conference room, then.

They approached stealthily.

"Smutt!"

Ah, so the Smutt Nadia knew as the man who never left Badmonkof's side was indeed the same Johann Smutt to whom Colby'd handed over sensitive information. At the moment, he had his hands halfway down the side of Ivle's leather briefcase.

"What are you doing?"

"Your husband keeps a list of condemned individuals—?"

"Oh yeah that's what we're looking for too—"

"I just, they told me to go— get—it," he came up for breath with his hands bunched in front of him like a gopher, clutching paper. The paper had a list of addresses on it.

"Yeah that's it! That's the paper we need,"

"Ivle told us to get it,"

"Ivle told me to get it,"

Ivle had, in fact, told neither of them to get it.

"What do you need it for?"

"Your husband claims Krakoveen owes the US 2 billion dollars."

"Oh—Cool. We're looking for one of my friend's cousins; I think he bought something from the US."

Dammit! Smutt should have known they wouldn't be up to anything influential enough to be worth knowing about. Now he'd told them too much.

"Can I just look at it—real fast for like one second?" Nadia made little grubby-fingers hand gestures towards him.

"Ah, I don't think— it's—state secrets."

"It's my house."

"Smutt hand it over." Visen was the one with the gun.

But it was Nadia who'd thought to bring along a sharpie.

"I just need to fix something very fast—" she looked down the list of names, searching. Nori had texted her precisely what name Desmond was looking for.

"Ah here we go; that's just wrong there I'm just going to go ahead and cross that out; it's a bit dated," lots of sharpie swished back and forth to obliterate the name.

"Ok! And then, also," she'd recognized someone from the country club, listed under 'Tax Evasion'—well Ivle did that too. Off the list they went. In all likelihood it wasn't even tax evasion they were wanted for…. More like political indiscretions,most likely.

"Alright, ah—, I'm just going to—" Smutt snagged the paper back from her, "thank you. Do you have a phone I could borrow?"

"There's one right there," Visen pointed at the desk beside her.

"No, I meant— more private. Is that possible?"

Why yes, Nadia had 26 faux ivory desk phones sprinkled throughout the mansion to choose from. She led Smutt into a little parlor of a maid's office, closed the door on her way back out, then bent to listen closely at its keyhole, signaling across the hall at Visen, who'd stayed put: 'find Badmonkof's copy! The— Badmonkof's copy!'

Lip reading was evidently not Visen's strong suit.

Then, when she finally did understand, there were over 36 briefcases in the room for her to choose from.

"I don't know which one!" she managed to gesture almost entirely using her face.

"Smutt?" Nadia straightened up to call out, "which one is Badmonkof's briefcase?"

"What?" he peered back out of the evidently not-so-private phoning room.

"Which one is Badmonkof's briefcase?"

"…why do you want to know?"

"Look, if you didn't see us, we didn't see you."

Nadia knew Ivle didn't trust Smutt enough to ask him to retrieve documents for him. No one trusted Smutt.

"It's the one at the end." Smutt popped back into seclusion, irritated.

"Thank youuuu," Nadia hurried back across the hall to where Visen had already started strategically combing through miscellaneous briefcases. "It's the one at the end—"

"Ah, the one at the end—"

They strategically combed.

"Oh wait—!"

"Oh yeah ok this looks like a list of people to kill," it had phone numbers and addresses.

"Check with," Visen nodded toward the scullery door, gesturing with her gun to indicate Smutt. Nadia nodded brightly and backtracked across the hall.

The phone on the other side of the scullery door had just connected. "Ah yes hello. Typical readout. Jacobs, Connor B. 257 Market Place. Reynolds, Aswold the fourth. 792 Henry Park Avenue…"

Those weren't the names Nadia'd just read off Ivle's list. She looked down at Badmonkof's copy. They weren't the names Badmonkof had received either. Reynolds was there, but not Jacobs.

Nadia hesitated, glancing between Visen and the door, scared to make a sound. Connor B. Jacobs had shot down every single word Smutt said the last time they'd interacted in Nadia's presence.

She might not know the politics behind it, but she could read the emotional aftermath. They weren't allies.

"Visen!" she hissed. "Visen! Come here!"

Visen could tell, at least, that Nadia was scared to interrupt Smutt.

"Hey!" Visen called, striding over to knock.

"What?! What is it?!" Smutt disconnected his private call.

"Is this the list of people the secret police want to get rid of?" They showed him Badmonkof's printout.

Visen cocked her gun to forestall equivocations right off the bat.

"Right…."

In political parlance this string of names was called a 'watch list' and 'people the secret police want to get rid of' were called saboteurs because that's what they were, and anyone caught claiming Swiverlia's government simply compiled an arbitrary hit list could find themselves on the next rendition. Seemed Visen hadn't been around long enough to care about the way she phrased things.

Smutt looked over Badmonkof's list at gun point. "Yeah. This is, uh— for October," he showed them the time stamp.

"Lemme see your list," Nadia tapped at the paper Smutt still held. They traded.

Nadia got out her phone and started taking pictures.

"What are you—?"

"I thought it could help!" she turned to Visen for support.

Visen was still the one with the gun.

Nadia continued taking pictures.

Finally: "Ok, thanks!"

Smutt snagged Ivle's list back and slunk into the maid's office, playing eye contact like daggers with Visen as though his life depended on it, until the mahogany door closed between them.

"Thought maybe the two lists might be different." Nadia grinned, apologetic. She was too used to her own hunches being disregarded to actually feel comfortable telling Visen she thought Smutt had doctored his own version of the list. After all, Smutt was the politician. He probably just knew more about what that list indicated than Nadia did.

But Visen, as always, was supportive. "Yeah, no, good point."

They turned to find a 65-year-old Mertrian cabinet member had appeared on the landing and was currently in the process of slinking into the conference room. "Ah...." He tried to seem very official. "Do you know which briefcase is Thompson's, by any chance?"

Oh Gawd.

"Yeah it's the, third one on the left," Visen remembered the moniker.

Nadia demanded they get pictures of what this gentleman was stealing as well. "Now we can blackmail him," she whispered, as soon as he'd left.

"Should we wait for anyone else?"

Nadia's face lit up at the thought of being included in an operation— (*Visen had said 'we'! Like—together, doing an operation!*) —at almost precisely the same instant her phone rang. "Oh damnit! —Hello?"

"Nadia." It was Ivle. "Galice Badmonkof has suffered quite a shock, I need you to come take care of her."

"But I'm not good at taking care of people,"

"Nadia! Just for once—be useful?"

"We'll be there sir!"

"Wait— am I on speaker phone? —Don't put me on speaker phone,"

"What? It's just Visen," Nadia hung up on him.

Visen called Wheeler to come guard the conference room.

~*~

Here ends *Fighting Fire Part 1: Collusion*. (Because it costs about 3$ less to print a book if you cut it in half —I'm hoping to drive down the paperback price!). To find out what happens next, look for *Fighting Fire Part 2: Rigged Elections* (available on Amazon; free with Kindle Unlimited at the time of publication).

So, Dear Reader, read on ☺